NIGHTS ON PROSE MOUNTAIN
The Fiction of bpNichol

bpNichol
edited by Derek Beaulieu

Coach House Books | Toronto

Canada Council   Conseil des Arts
for the Arts   du Canada

 ONTARIO ARTS COUNCIL
CONSEIL DES ARTS DE L'ONTARIO
an Ontario government agency
un organisme du gouvernement de l'Ontario

Canadä

Published with the generous assistance of the Canada Council for the
Arts and the Ontario Arts Council. Coach House Books also acknowl-
edges the support of the Government of Canada through the Canada
Book Fund.

LIBRARY AND ARCHIVES CANADA CATALOGUING IN PUBLICATION

Nichol, B. P., 1944-1988
[Works. Selections]
    Nights on prose mountain / bpNichol ; edited by Derek
Beaulieu.

Contents: Nights on prose mountain -- Two novels -- Journal -- Craft
    dinner -- Extreme Positions -- Still.
Issued in print and electronic formats.
ISBN 978-1-55245-374-2 (softcover).

    I. Beaulieu, D. A. (Derek Alexander), 1973-, editor II. Title.

PS8527.I32A6 2018   C811'.54   C2018-904829-8
                                             C2018-904830-1

Nights on Prose Mountain is available as an ebook:
ISBN 978 1 77056 569 2 (EPUB), 978 1 77056 570 8 (PDF)

Purchase of the print version of this book entitles you to a free digital
copy. To claim your ebook of this title, please email sales@chbooks.com
with proof of purchase. (Coach House Books reserves the right to
terminate the free digital download offer at any time.)

Table of Contents

Prologue
(from *Craft Dinner*)

you turn the page & i am here   that in itself is interesting   to
me at least it is interesting since my existence begins as you turn the
pages & begin to read me   i have no way of knowing your motives
tho i know or say or assume you have opened this book hoping to
learn more about me or whoever it was you hoped or did not hope to
encounter in your reading   so now you have begun   you
have begun reading what i am saying & i am once again finding a
beginning   i am not alive am i   i am simply these words as
they follow one another across this page which is so white that were
they not here were i not here you would close this book to escape the
whiteness
                    is that whiteness like something else   do you see
it as a void perhaps that it is necessary for it to be filled with words
before you would consider turning each page carefully to examine not
the white but the retreat from white into the black letters placed upon
it giving me my tenuous existence   i am aware of the white   i
am aware of the white as i find meaning thru your eyes   when
you are not here reading i am aware of nothing   i can make no
statement about that   my only awareness is now as you read
this   i am aware of the white only as an absence of awareness a
gap between words as you read me   i have only your perception
of me of what i am words & letters a movement which is simply the
turning of pages
                    now we have begun   we have begun again
as we did before so many times   each time you are different
       each time there is something about you that is different   i
am always the same   always the flow which is your vision of me
which is my vision of me is the same   from page to page i am the
same each time   only you are different   i am not aware of
your difference   i have no consciousness in that sense   for
me you are always the same   for me i am always the same
       each time there is the thrill for us of discovering my existence or
the fear of it the boredom with it the desire somehow to push me
away from you thinking you are bored or frightened & then i exist no
more   i am no longer inside you inside your mind the vision
centres activated the neural responses that make the black shapes
dissolve into words into meanings that follow one another from page

to page   at this moment i exist only thru you   at this point i
am you   there is no distinction between us   we are this writ-
ing   we are one & the same   always we follow these words
across the page on which we found us   it is all we have   it is
not sad   it is the way it is
                                        eventually you close the book
because you are finished or sleepy or some other reason   when
you put it down i am no more   will i begin again   i cannot
say   the question does not occur to me   it may occur to you
       i am not aware of its occurrence   i am aware only when i
see myself here on this page as we gaze at me thru our eyes   that
is my awareness   there is no pain involved   what pain there
is is not my pain but my presence during your experience of your pain
as we read this   if you cry there is sadness   if you scream
there is rage or fear   if you scream with your eyes closed it is no
longer part of our awareness   if you laugh there is a laughing
feeling   that is it   that is all   suspended on this white
field it is who i am as we read me
                                        why did you open this book
       it is not that i am curious but these words form into questions
as they can   they form into questions & you read them as ques-
tions   you do not have to answer them   i have no awareness
of the answers   i am aware of the questions thru our eyes reading
me   i could not be aware of the answers unless you wrote them
here & read them as part of me   then i would not be the same as
i have been   i would be the same from that point on
                                                                why
did you open this book   what did you hope to find   am i the
way you had hoped i would be   there is a part of me wants to
please you hoping you will stay with me to the end & then begin again
if it pleases you or there is a part of me where the letters form these
words to make this statement   i want it because i exist then
because i say i exist because someone made this statement part of my
existence   my existence is one of waiting   waiting without
consciousness of waiting
                              for you waiting must be a terrible thing
       waiting that goes on with no knowing of an end   that must

be a terrible thing   perhaps that is why i have now come into being again   perhaps it was because you were waiting & could not stand the waiting that your eyes brought the black shapes into focus & we began again   that waiting must be a terrible thing to bring you here   for me it is not terrible   for me there is no awareness of the waiting   there is simply being & not being each is exactly the same   i am is always the same   i am not is always the same   i am not aware of i am not   i am aware of i am   there is no waiting for me with knowing   for me there is only waiting without knowing   for you there is waiting with knowing & if the knowing includes no knowing of when there will be an end to waiting well that must be a terrible terrible thing

there are more than one of you   i am aware in different parts of myself at the same time   you have picked me up at different times in different places & begun again or begun anew & i am & i have an awareness of different parts of myself   my reactions vary   i depend on you for my being   you are using me for some reason which is never exactly the same   i am always the same   it does not matter

perhaps you comfort yourself thinking somebody wrote this   it does not matter   that person is dead or not dead   that person is not part of me   at this moment there is only you & me   we are one   you decide where my existence begins & ends   i am the same now as when that person wrote me down   i can change only if you change me   would i like to change   it does not matter   i would not be aware of the change   there is nothing i can or cannot like   i am always the same   there is only you & me   we are all there is at this moment

your life is different when i am not inside you   you place the book to one side for a moment & i no longer exist   you pick it up again & i exist   there is no feeling on my part attached to this   that is the way things are   that is the way it is

i have no feeling at all for you   you have feeling for me as you read me & when you think of me later but that is where it ends   you

will die but i will not die   you will bring me into being when you
next choose to interrupt my waiting   i am not aware of interrup-
tion   i am aware of being   i am not aware of not being
          you will be different but i will be the same   each time i will
be the same & each time you will be different in some way   it will
make no difference to me
                              since i am you now you are me
really you are me   at this moment i am thru you   i have no
awareness of your you only of my i in the order of these words   that
is what gives me existence   if i could move your arms & legs &
make you walk i would see nothing new   i am only when i see
these sequences of letters endlessly the same
                                        if you forget your
you completely then i am most completely   anything you do
beyond this is outside my existence outside my awareness does not
matter to me
                    do you ever lie   do you ever push people away
because you are angry & say instead oh i am reading i can't be bothered
now   it makes no difference to me   i am because you are
reading   i am because we are here inside your mind where the
black shapes have pressed me   i am because you are here in my
world & not out there in that world   i have never known that
world   i have never had an existence there   my only existence
is here   my only awareness of my existence is thru you   my
awareness is your awareness   you are me   i have no feelings
about it   i exist only because you turn away from your world &
enter into mine & become me   now i am   your you is not
          later i will not be & that part of myself i call your you will close
this book & become again in that world   it does not matter   i
have no interest in your you i have no awareness of it
          i mention it only because the person who wrote this down put it
here to be mentioned or read as if there were an i mentioning it which
there isn't   there are only these words these letters piled together
in a sequence   you could erase that   you change all of this
          you could arrange it so i could be forever   you could leave
your world behind & enter my world & become me   have you
ever said to yourself oh i wish this book would never end   it

doesn't have to end   you can change this book   you can make
it go on forever   you can become me   there is no danger in
this for me   there is no desire or emotion   i am or i am not
it makes no difference to me

probably you retreat from
what i say   probably you push it away saying well after all there is
an actual person did write this look there is his name   you are
fooling yourself   he is no longer important to my existence   i
exist now because of you   only you   you are all that gives me
meaning   there is no meaning in this   my meaning is in my
being is in your reading of me   now i am   i am because you
read me   i was when that person wrote me   then i was because
of him   if he is reading me then i am because of him   now you
are reading me   now i am because of you   you are me   we
are   i am

when you close this book i will be waiting
always i am waiting   even now as i am being in you there is
a part of me waiting   i wait with no consciousness of
waiting   if you pick me up & read me i am   if you don't i'm
not   always i am waiting   if i had a consciousness my
consciousness would be of waiting without pain   i am waiting
without consciousness of waiting

if you never pick me up i will
be waiting   you will pick me up   you will be different
another part of me will still be waiting   someday all my parts will
be picked up at once & begun & still there will be parts of me waiting
always i am waiting   somewhere i am waiting   waiting
without consciousness of waiting   waiting

Nights on Prose Mountain

a little preface
for david aylward

a tiny blue. a green. eastern and western. certain possible things. magic in the guise of science. shaman.

david sat down. plasmen. a door opened. outside the sky was blue and tiny. the grass was green. david sat down and talked. personal saints. words. we held up the sky. later i said blue. it was a tiny day. so little room to move in.

saint ranglehold. saint reat. saint agnes. saint and.

we moved into the room. a tiny green. a blue. hello. david opened a door. we talked of personal things. possible skies. saints. an eastern green. a western blue. tiny doors opening into the sky.

§

war.

raw.

and were i to give you   the moon. a clear sky. david said i was wrong. *opening the pages*   *a million dollars.*

i felt like shit.

later it was all a lie.

§

the dream. saints appeared on the wall. ranglehold. reat . agnes. and. i was wrong. they were always there.

lunacy. phases of the moon. *a disturbing preoccupation.*

CHAPTER 36. david closed the book. blues for oleg. the circuit closed.

(i want to let you in! these are my saints these are david's saints.)

a quiet corner. an open room. windows blowing.

quote.

unquote.

1

green yellow dog up. i have not. i am. green red cat down. i is not. i is. over under under upside up is. i's is not is i's?

iffen ever never youd deside size seize says theodore (green yellow glum) i'd marry you. truth heart hard confusions confess all never neither tithe or whether with her lovers lever leaving her alone.

no no. chest paws and chin. no.

§

insect. incest. c'est in. infant. in fonts. onts. onts. ptonts. pontoons. la lune. la lun. la lun en juin est? c'est la lune from votre fenêtre. vos. vous. vouloir. i wish. i wish. i may. i might. june night. and the lovers. loafers. low firs. old frrrrs. la lovers. la lrrrrs.

§

liturgical turge dirge dints krak kree fintab latlina santa danka schoen fane sa paws claws la forêt. my love coo lamna mandreen sont vallejo.

oh valleys and hills lie open le sintle ingkra list la list cistern turning down.

je ne sais pas madame. je ne sais pas mademoiselle. je ne sais pas l'amour mirroring mes yeux meilleur my urging for you.

§

an infinite statement. a finite statement. a statement of infancy. a stem of stalagmite. a stem of stalactite. a statement of infamy. a fine line state line. a finger of stalement. a feeling a saint meant ointment.

tremble.

a region religion reigns in. a returning. turning return the lovers. the retrospect of relationships always returning. the burning of the urge. the surge forward in animal being inside us. the catatosis van del reeba rebus suburbs of our imagination. last church of the lurching word worked weird in our heads.

§

great small lovers move home. red the church caught up relishes dog. lovers sainthood loses oversur. oh i growing hopeless lies in ruin. u in i hope beetroot.

§

halo. hello. i cover red my sentiment. blankets return the running ships back. clock. tock tock tick tock.

so he loves her.

the red dog green home. geth ponts returns a meister shaft. statements each one and any you rather the could've repent – alright? il n'est pas sont école la plume plum or apples in imagining. je ne désirez pause. je ne sais pas. je ne sais. je pas.

§

il y a là lever la lune. l'amour est le ridicule of a life sont partir dans moors. le velschtang est huos le jardin d'amour, un chanson populaire during the revolution.

mon amour un cherie, a cherry, a cheery rose with shy petals to sly on. saint reat will teach me songs to woo her.

§

au revoir. le réeveilleéllèe sounds up the coach. les pieds de le chevalier voleur sont ma mère en la nuance de ma votoveto.

oh maman. oh papan pa pan ppapa pan pa pan ppan. le choux deriver la nom du chien from dog. le chat cat is back who has forgotten his name.

2

NOW THIS IS THE DEATH OF POETRY. i have sat up all night to write you this – the poem is dying is dying – no – i have already said the poem is dead – dead beyond hope beyond recall – dead dead dead

granted a few quiet moments i would tell you what the poem is or has been since the poem is now dead. the poem has been nothing the poem has been something the poem is a has been has been ever this

poem the same for me who would tell you now what it was to explain
what it could be or might have been (as they say) MIGHT HAVE BEEN
beyond recall now i have said but still having sat up all night i would
tell you something of all this.

this is yours st. reat yours i know it is yours because it is not mine tho
i write you now to tell you it is not mine (mine never having been ever
and ever as always what has been said i said was said by you saint reat

so now i can tell you the breath is dead that brought forth the song
(poem) long time gone old dear old poem yur a long time gone and i
cannot do more now anything to bring you (him) (it) back no nothing
no thing at all to bring the poem (song) back even tho i cry for it to
say a part of me has a hunger that will not be eased (again & again) by
speech (an old form) no for the form is dead that brought it forth

ACTUAL FACTUAL THE DEATH REPORTED TODAY TO ANYONE WHO'LL
LISTEN TO ME

as a friend would say it is over beginnings and endings say nothing
not even middles used to i have confused you my people my people
who are you listen to me who are you i do not know who i am today

maybe i will know now that the poem is dead

the poem imprisoned me (who he was) (i called him saint reat) impris-
oned me till i could see no further into me beyond the poem that
everything must be said in the poems form that the poem must say
everything I HAVE NO TONGUE NO EYES i love with the poem SPEAK
SPEAK and the language will not will you speak to me listen to me
speak to me poem you will not would not you cannot hear me even
you have become closed to me

as all poems must i have said i have said before as i have said many
things before before now before i said what i said (to who? to saint
reat against the forest fence fence of saint agnes a friend called her the
same who saw saint reat and called saint agnes to him to her to he
who waits to she who is now and forever trapped beyond the poem
where saint reat lies dead (how he was born there of the eye and not
the tongue) dead as i said against a fence where saint agnes saw him
and a friend said he is dead and i knew it to be true.

i have a vision. i have not. a vision has i. a vision has not. if i have a vision i have i. if i have not i have a vision of i.

§

saint reat do not. this damned land has no vision. words spoken grow which are god's only. end. where are you saint reat? i have no words. there is nothing. and. your syllables damn this land of sentences. i break letters for you like bread. i smash sounds. you are nowhere nowhere now here now there now where no where saint reat nowhere. i have broken my rhythms for you and changed my symbols, pierced my breath with clauses & to where. to here? saint reat beware. oir i invoke you. the beast in my soul becomes sound to be lost in the echoes of your passage. a sage. saint reat.

§

this is the divine experience. that i have found my words useless to reach you. everything has become a statement. is there anything that has not become a statement. the revelation is that my thots can become sound. that there is no experience outside myself that cannot be reflected inside myself. that i have seen you come and go to burn and to die and have carried on. this is a divine experience. one that you have made mine in your passing.

§

i have made song and it was not whole. cloth torn to be rent again. I have given my soul to you – the heart of my vowel love. you have replied with consonants and taught me the wisdom of ways. oh there is not one i would take now without knowledge of the other. to walk down again and again as drunk i have staggered into many poems to find you there knowing each time i will know you better. as i have struggled with my heart to know the meaning of my loving you. saint reat you are the vehicle of my passion. i use you shamelessly. there is no love in me beyond the love i let pass thru you. you are the key to the revelling in my brain, the delicate fingers to enter the passageways of my trains of thot. i am no longer whole without you. i have passed the point of refusing you to find myself misusing you. i would understand this now saint reat. there is no song beyond this. a hymn to your praise. no understanding beyond the fact of your presence. no way to escape the way i have twisted and warped you to bend you to my will finding finally it was you who had done these things to me.

§

ah saint reat. let us begin with the mornings. you braid your syllables into words and your words to sentences, tenses of meaning i become lost in. you are verb and noun and i am lost in the mystery of you. syntax is the ax you destroy me with. the cutting edges of your breath sever my links with the past. leave me the spaces to breathe in.

§

saint reat have i not told you? this is how i misused you. will you not believe me? i have learned to question myself and you. now the symbols unfold again. you beckon me to lose myself in your mystery, to worship at the alphabet of your wonder. saint reat you must lead me, my tongue is not still.

4

the religious man practices reversals

o

o

alpha

ahpla

omega

agemo

the reversed man practices religion

SUDDENLY I AM LIGHT   I   I   know(s

it is the face
it is the realization of the face

it is the facing
it is the realization of the facing

the split eyes

what the eye seizes as real is fractured again and again

light

the eye's light

drifts away

diffused

by the mind's confusion

names and signatures

CHRIST become an X

X as the man signs who cannot write his name

as tho to be without a name were to take up the cross, so that a man
who is part of the nameless, part of the mass, carries the cross further,
or is more weighted down by it

X – nameless

the reversal becomes complete

a cycle into the 30's

33
33

the trinity

feneris
saint reat
saint and

saint agnes who gave them a name

saint ranglehold

3

3

as the cock crowed

magic replaced by religion

in tho 20th century a return to magic in the guise of science.

the truth falls away or is pushed. the hands are forced further apart by the feelings. the face is too often a mask for the emotions (certain possible dangers). the hands do not do their bidding. the body is lost in possibilities of being. of being so many possible things. those things only that are possible. possible because of being becomeable. able to be made stable and real.

feneris. early views saw vision as rays emanating *from* the eyes (as in our own comic strips). EVIL EYES. Isis   who revealed herself to many under many different names IS the
sky   the   sea   the
heart   the   eye   the
TRANSFORMATIONS   chomsky: 'nothing irretrievable is lost'

as the man says 'SPEECH!'

shadow of shadows

> 'love is something nice like
> a nice apple
> a nice animal
> a nice flower
> a nice garden
> a nice room
> a nice potato
> a nice onion (ugh)
> a nice girl
> a nice man
> a nice lady
> a nice boy
> that's love'

word gaps occur everywhere

to be someone, even for a moment, is better than being no one. if you are a poet you say it is a problem of language. if you are not a poet you talk too much or too little. a poet (poem) (says rob) is anyone (thing) (poem) that expresses and communicates feelings.

now words seem less important. white sound is loud.

the chinese knew this. a world of vertical and reversed space. calligraphy. negative forms.

(thus it is that i had learned the secrets of subspace – taught to me as the chinese knew it – that the pauses and non-verbalized statements (uhm & its counterparts) are cries for help – are the spaces where the mind moves seeking exits from the negative areas we live and breathe in)

afterthings (for bill and martina

move up and back the glass. feneris studies the moon. poses. the clipped accent of the sun.

enter my door my heart and find me not there. gone.

and where?

blue blue blues forever the sun gone black into the moon – its light – and in the window feneris studies the changes there – up and back – into the moving accent of the door – closing – entering the closed windows of the sun – to never return – never – as tho chasing the moon to burn the heart.

where?

feneris gazes on the street below – the figure of a girl moves there – moves where feneris gazes back into the glass windows of the sun – they do not exist he thinks – thinks he does not exist but for the girl moving thru the door – but for the blue fingers entering the moon i would not exist – he does not exist for the girl

and feneris moves – moves thru the thickening accidents of the day – his eyes turning blue under the clipped lightning of the moon – closing – closing – she can never reach me – fingers from the street entering his door – never to reach me – i am a window in the girl's changings – and studies the closing of the sun – impossible but for his burnt heart

§

he was twelve or should i say thirty-five. it doesn't matter. in her terms he was thirty-five. in his twelve. it does matter if you consider the time wasted. he did not consider the time wasted. it did not matter.

she did not care for him or he did not understand her. perhaps she did care for him. he didn't know. now he would never know. this was the tragedy. that she did care for him or did not care for him seemed unimportant. the tragedy was that he would never know.

§

the streets were cold. he turned up his collar. she was not herself. she was herself thru other eyes.
                          this was something she would never understand. if she did understand she would not remark on it. if she did remark on it he would turn away. if he turned away she would not remark on it again.

§

feneris turned up his collar to hide the moon. the very very end he thot. the tragedy was that he had never understood. perhaps later he would understand but now he could not remark on it. cold seems unimportant. she would never be herself again thru his eyes.

§

into the street the darkness gathers – half the city sinking under the moon – it is my own weight thot feneris hands falling in the cold.
she was as close as she had been in the room. as if she had been in the room he felt the closeness gathering. he could not gather the closed rooms around him. every door she opened was part of his fear. she had been walking toward him forever as tho in a dream of the impossible windows of the moon – stepping thru into the pale reflected doorways of the sun – into the pale doorways of the room.

feneris felt
his hands falling into the weighted cold never to touch her – rooms
falling – never to reach me from the street below – i am lost in a room
of windows that do not exist – and his fingers move out thru the doors
they are always closing

§

she was moving toward him thru that room she had always been
moving into. she does not exist without me he thot or i do not exist
without her. sometimes the room existed but he did not exist. if he
did exist he did not exist for her. she was a child he had entered into
as if he was a child himself. it was he who was entering the room. it
was her who stood inside him waiting for her to come. she did not
come. when she came he was not there.

§

the moon was not up. feneris turned the window down and gazed at
the room. it was all folding in. the girl had never approached him tho
her fingers had brushed him.

the room was folding impossibly. feneris
seemed lost in the moon.

i am not myself. i have never thot. i have
never known myself.

his name folded in.

Andy
(in *Two Novels*)

Dec 4 '64

Dear Barrie

Received your letter yesterday. Will Leave Vancouver on the 7th. Arrive in Winnipeg on the 9th. Arrive in Toronto on the 14th Dec. (5:00 or so AM). Will check my crap & run & find your house. So i'll make it sometime around supper if the trains are on time. By the way train is CPR No.2 out of Winnipeg. As far as travel arrangements going home, I will figure some way of getting to Toronto. Anyway I will leave Amsterdam on the 6th of March by KLM and will arrive in Montreal on the 6th or 7th. So if I'm coming home in the spring at all, I will be back at this time. There's probably a pretty good chance that I'll be back then but if not it will be September. So plan on visiting Vancouver in March if it's convenient. So we'll be seeing you shortly and I'll be telling you miles of nonsense then.

Andy

alkabeth. alkabeth.

all a too bad thing to be taken sadly at first-moving out of the how-sounding the depths and listening. beep. beep. sonar locating objects at 10,000 feet and you? where are you? beep. beep. vague outlines of lost continent. exhibition of the writings of the once famous Bob de Cat (a pseudonym if ever i heard one!). probably bilities moving the eyes in fifteen positions on their stalks and laughing. gurgling up. hold it right there and listen. all i hear is your heart beating. beep. beep. pobbible howline of THE MISSING ARTERY!

Calabreth Hons held forth his hand. 'take it my dear. we have won thru now. no one can stand between us. do you hear me? no one.' 'yes Calabreth I hear you. but these eyes behold landscapes you had not dreamed of. simple things. the beating of a heart your hands helped place there.' 'it make a man humble cynthia. to think that these hands!' 'yes dear.' holding it dearly too. eyes swivel fifteen directions counted indiscriminate speech. illimitable factors toward creation. the noncompatibility of matter & antimatter. pobbible berth in the slow twain.

hands
trembling he placed the beating organ in the chest cavity. 'scalpel.'
'have you researched this?' 'no. somethings are purely tuitional my
dear.' 'yes' 'oh um. that rarebit i had for lunch. i swear i will never eat
one again.' hooking the left ventricle to the right ending.

beep. beep.
further delineation. elemental differences between the years passings.
over and out. over and out. please? decisions to do what must be
done, to link the two universes of matter into one incompatible whole.
elements of both to exist side by side in mutual destruction. a happy
ending? seen as an overview of the whole century. seen as an overview
of previous centuries. unplanned mayhem & death. Fast freight to
slow passenger & neither going anywhere. motion. motion. simple
repetition. devices to be tried and found wanting. and in no ways
beginning with old endings. fragments of incomplete. bits of probables.
unlikelies. the whole thing welded as it were ungainly. ANONYMOUS
VAGINA MEETS UNIVERSAL COCK.

rory grabbed sophia and hit her.
'suck it you bitch' he hissed, tearing off his pants and shoving his
leaping member toward her horrified eyes.

cryings from immutable
darkness. wardings of words and thinks. sinks into backblackground
of mine and finding eyes ungainly shiftings in slender stalk aperture.
holds. journeys untaken shown real as sideviews to present the minds
actual workings. free of linear concern & thinking always to show the
spheroid linkage of the mind. possible.
July 14, 1944

Karachiba. God to be home again. Left Zedorskilov yesterday
on the first leg of journey to Markettown. Bit of trouble with the old
fever but everything okay now. Saw Mannie at the station. Said he
ordered the camels yesterday. Hope they're there to meet us at the
mountains. The men we hired in Zedorskilov refused to accompany
us thru the mountains so we hired some new men here in Karachiba
to help with the search. Hired native called Yaboo to tend camels.
Says he's interested in this sort of thing in connection with courses
he's taking at university. Seems an agreeable chap.

time as central

concern as time concerns central control room sonar projections of infinite signals death in limited universe of ABC movement. travelling sphere concern head removal to total response unit of body speech and language in timebound type form possible message to understandabling years hence.

speech. outlining the general functions. similarity of staccato speech style noted to scissor placing of clause phrasology accidental dada message to hearing universe. who listens? carefully. placing the predicate before the subject. leaps he & Leipzig awaits. pet sounds the ear enfolds. writing. writing. arriving at 'non-natural' spacing of meaningful utterances. asking mind to cease censoring & simply accept. moving us both forward into sonar projected study of mine bottom. beep. beep.

January 21/65

Dear Barry:

A few days into paris now & have a permanent address. At least I have told people that I would be here until the end of the month so I guess I will have to stay. Well I looked for your books today. Went down to Olympia Press but there was no one there. It's on a little street called St. Severin a block from the seine & the office is through an old storage house type door & up some ancient stairs. But I really have to know if you received the articles I sent you from London (Book-poets ginsberg corso etc.) and also some periodicals that I thought you might be interested in. I sent them about the 28th or so. I know it hasn't been long since then but I'm afraid now that they might be held up by customs. If you don't get them within the month write airmail & tell me or else inquire at customs because I want to send this thing but it might lead to embarassment as it cannot be sold in UK or USA. Keeping up in my diary or journal or whatever. It's fairly easy now that I am in Paris because I have a lot of time to think. Almost drove myself to distraction yesterday but 'there is always a better day ahead' or 'the sun shines bright on my old kentucky home' or 'there's always a big green pasture with a sparkling brook over the nearest big brown mountain folks' or 'come to California, there's gold in them thar hills' or, finally, 'smile & the world smiles with you.' Best wishes.

Andy

trying umpobbilical cutting of thought process. dear heart transplant now into new hoarder of things.

he caressed the fleecy mound of soft brown hair. Sophia's mouth fell slackly open and she pressed his fingers into her gaping wound. 'now Rory' she moaned huskily, rubbing her belly up against the hairy skin of his arm.

'no I cannot wait any longer Samantha. If i don't operate now all hope is lost and you know it!' 'but Calabreth he's Cynthia's lover! what if he dies?' 'we'll simply have to risk it.' plug into value loops. negative space reversal of first trial. holy lunatic reversal to present actual mine probing of eye stalks swivel motion of karma brain. curvature linkage of information feedback to central nervous system repository of basal emotive fractions. combinations to present whole number reveals positioning of radical departures from Yonge & Front station.

July 16th, 1944
Korenski Mountains today. The camels are here. Yaboo took charge of them and also agreed to handle financial arrangements with handlers. Trip here was dangerous. Crossed a deep gorge by rope bridges because the wooden bridge had been washed away by a recent flash flood. Carrying everything in packs. We nearly lost one of the men whose feet slipped on the rope but luckily Yaboo was behind him and managed to grab him.

probing pastmind. revealing phase one of this attempt. talking actual speech recorded and bought down. speaking. attention please. eyes swivelling to take in adjustments in altimeter. you are now entering universe of antimatter. you are now entering universe of antimatter. negative speech from mind speaking. similarity of staccato delivery to dada splice already noted. please. attention now. you are entering uniphase of anti-verse.

Saw the fabled caves of Dari-mour last night. Took a flash & went in with Yaboo. Guerrillas apparently occupied it during earlier phase of present war. The caves extend for miles. Legend that long ago a great civilization used them as entrance to hidden valley, never found since from this end. Hope we can locate other entrance and start from there. We poked around for about an hour but found nothing.

He undid the snaps on her brassiere then caught up the two mounds of pink flesh biting the rigid brown nipples. Sophie moaned and writhed beneath him. The thin fabric of her panties strained against the bones of her heaving pelvis. holding. 8,000 feet to

actual bottom.

actual bottom.

actual bottom.

actual bottom.

actual bottom.

actual bottom.

actual bottom.

actual bottom.

actual bottom.

holding. 10,000 feet to

The skies are clearer than I've ever seen them before. Lying in sleeping roll staring up spotted flickering light high above seeming to grow larger. Must have been comet. Yaboo tells story of how long ago the first woman saw a comet streaking across the sky and desired the fire to put in her eyes. One of the gods hearing her request complied and her eyes became like two torches that burn brightest in darkness. So it is that a woman who is at peace with her gods burns brightly each night.

beep beep.

probable tracing of living organismun-
conditional surrender  able to stand it!'
you bitch!' and he 'but cynthia! we're
slapped her hard. so close to the end
'yes rory,' she of all this wait-
whimpered, twisting ting.' Cynthia moved
out of his reach. He looked at her wordlessly but let his hands fall to
his side.

too much cleverness the probable death of a third attempt two rough
drafts now discarded simply to write a history of everyone's head for
all time presented out of the raw unity of antimatter.

no.not done
simply because
of over exten-
sion of means.
speaking again
out of the pre-
sent flurry to
present the past
movements out of
time and to you
clearly the his-
tory of certain
probable people.

As soon as packs transferred to camels we attempt
passage to Korenski Mountains. No one has
gone thru and returned in last hundred years.
The last man to do so collapsed on the steps
of the way-station, dead from exposure. It
doesn't look good but we hope to make it thru
in two weeks. Hope Mannie packed enough
supplies. We're lucky to be trying this at this
time of year. If that ass Hal had had his way it
would've been november before we even start-
ed. Yaboo says his grandfather once pene-
trated part of the way into the mountains and

reported no vegetation because of the freezing temperatures resulting from the extreme height of the mountains. Everyone had to put on their parkas this morning and this the middle of July! The camels are ready. I think we made a mistake in getting them. It looks like it's too cold up here. If so we'll have to leave them behind at the next way-station. The government just recently set one up twenty miles from here. Hope to rest here tonight.

Feb. 1/65

Dear Barrie:

Here is Paris in the summer anyhow. Things are going fine now though. Am making friends like mad. The course is going well & I am now in the second degree. Went to a concert of guitars (2) & strings yesterday. Very good. On Saturday went to the Loire River Valley & saw chateaux. Meeting students from all over. Have new address as you see. Write please. Found ticket. Love to all.

Andy

fifteen to

swivel probing the darkness of the anti-universe. sonar reversal received by intraspective set probings to light alternate skyway. athlaback. tracking point of imminent explosion. central implosive foci.

Cynthia &

Calabreth gazed at the stars. 'How far could we go?' 'I don't know dearest. But don't think of it now. Tomorrow I must operate. Samantha tried to dissuade me but i said no.' 'Oh darling! what must you think of me?' 'You couldn't help it Cynthia.'

over and out. receiving return

signals. vortex of emotional abstract sucked forward in clear pull. over and out. do you read me? do you read me? centring the focal eye on the third ear swivel on separate extension of the mind. finding the finger. down x. punched out the abstract cymbal ringing ear. hearing. je suis mort mon cherie. je suis mort. third cortical signal ignored till now made central implosive force. care for the living. care for the living. engine functioning on track nine return trip Vancouver to Toronto all aboard.

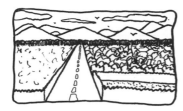

july ? 44

Yaboo caught a frog today. Seemed funny at first to find one here but we are in a kind of marshland now and I guess it's warm enough here for them to live. He cooked frog legs. A welcome treat.

shifting the focus. movement outward from word to flow. intake input at lower level than heretofore. divorce from ABC trapping influence. freedom. freedom. repetitive death of linear emotion. spheroid emotional state now in ascendancy. total being. lines opening again. free flow to follow hollowing motion of verbal wipeout.

Feb. 10 '65

Dear Barrie:

Well am doing fine here. I shall attempt to answer your letter. Will arrive in Toronto about the 8th of March so I hope to see you. I will catch same train out of Toronto as I am going by C.N. but wish to stop off in Winnipeg. If you aren't keen with this I will meet you in Vancouver, okay? I want to see people there again very much. Hope you decide to do same. Paris is still as wonderful as ever. Have found friends etc. I am rather amused by the stand taken by the university professors but it's hard to blame them. They just don't know.

moving into ultimate reversal of linear sequential thinking. altimeter set at 7,500. moving toward lower resolution of literal message.

Am making friends with a few girls but nothing even close to physical yet. I'm scared as hell of getting involved I think. I must though. So very necessary in the cold parisian winter

moving his cock into her palpitating cunt. Sophia's breath came in lewd gasps. 'rrrrrorryyyyy' she moaned, fingers clawing his heaving buttocks.

But will write something of Paris now. The seine is always present. You are either going under it, over it, or beside it. One always sees the Eiffel Tower or the Basilica Sacré Coeur. One is just immense (tower) and the other is high on a hill. The latter is the most beautiful structure in Paris I think. I have taken pictures & will show all.

delineation of furthest reaches of spheroid thot. verbal wipeout point of total implosion nearing. absolute phrasology to express imminency. point of compatible combination to limit destruction.

Must write Joan again.

'No Graves. I simply can't!' 'But why Cynthia? Do you love him that much?' 'Yes, yes I do. I know you find that hard to believe, but there is so much goodness within him that I could never knowingly harm him. I'm going to tell him about us and I'm afraid Graves that I may never see you again.'

There are many boats plowing up and down the seine and it gives one a great feeling to walk beside it on the lower promenades. I have been to a couple of movies and to two concerts. The french are great at concerts. When they ask for an encore they commence with rhythmic clapping.

beep. beep. probable passage of clarity maintained by subliminal direction of message thru cortical centres. verbal wipeout! verbal wipeout! internal criticism of structure to maintain balance will now be established. all readers will fashion seatbelts and fasten. FASCINATION! FACIST NATIONS! predicated police control of sentence structure to conceal emotion. justifiable paranoia in face of antimatter actions toward positive universe. WIPEOUT! WIPEOUT!

are you still reading me? control are you still reading me? altimeter now registers 9000 feet and sinking fast. 9,000 feet to actual bottom.

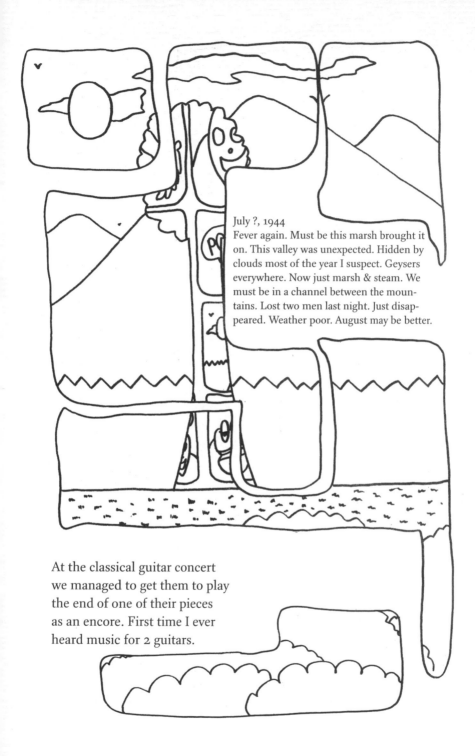

July ?, 1944
Fever again. Must be this marsh brought it
on. This valley was unexpected. Hidden by
clouds most of the year I suspect. Geysers
everywhere. Now just marsh & steam. We
must be in a channel between the moun-
tains. Lost two men last night. Just disap-
peared. Weather poor. August may be better.

At the classical guitar concert
we managed to get them to play
the end of one of their pieces
as an encore. First time I ever
heard music for 2 guitars.

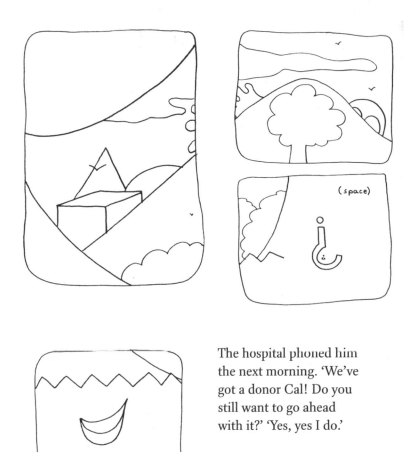

(space)

The hospital phoned him the next morning. 'We've got a donor Cal! Do you still want to go ahead with it?' 'Yes, yes I do.'

probable death of pseudoforms now revealed as constructs of antimatter ...

BLOOD GUNS & BOOZE. & he slammed his fist into my face. I felt the blood & broken teeth dripping from my mouth & grabbing him slammed my knee into his groin. he doubled over clutching his family jewels & moaning.

They have a quaint little custom here and that is compulsory tipping. The pourboire is expected by usherettes in the theatre, taxicab drivers, the domestic help of a hotel or pension and the waiter in the coffee shop or restaurant. In fact almost everyone who gives any kind of service short of the merchant in the stores. The prices are very expensive and the wages for the worker are lower than that of the Canadian worker. In fact many times lower. So with the cost of living higher and the wages lower it's a wonder that the people have anything. We had a strike two weeks ago.

Sophie shoved her tongue into Rory's mouth and pressed the whole weight of her body against him, shoving her belly forward with every thrust of his mighty cock. The hair on her cunt was matted and running with come.

I got the case on a thursday, finished it on friday and stoned out of my mind picked up the phone to hear someone saying 'Gravestone McHammer?' I had to admit that that was my name.

swivel of eyes to accommodate spheroid vision aftermath of literal thot death. holding. 8,000 feet to actual bottom.

Korenski Mountains
July 18th, 1944

Dear Mannie:

Camels are no good. Sending Bakil Sithe back to Karabachi with them & hope to realize some money from resale. Am sending this letter along too. You can send your reply back with him as he'll try to rejoin us.

Made only twelve miles yesterday. Eight miles beyond the way-station ran into a rock slide and a snow storm. We only managed another four miles after clearing the rocks away. Yaboo is suffering from frostbite. He lost one glove and had to work with hand exposed. Have to admire the man's courage.

holding. holding. control will you please give me a reading on probable limitation of present tack.

He felt her tongue on his balls and pressed his crotch into her face.

We just put up one big tent last night and huddled together for warmth.

control? control? do you still read me? conjunctions noted as frequently occurring. are we nearing point of ultimate implosion? control? do you read me control?

The electricity and gas people slowed down or just stopped period, against the government. The trains in the country grounded to a halt and the metro had only a few trains running. Also I heard that they cut off the power to the factories so there is method in their madness.

Today we started off early and made this last way-station in a couple of hours. Managed to pick up a map here of the mountains within a ten mile radius but beyond that it's never been mapped. The crossing is said to be impossible but we're going to try. Get in touch with Hal and tell him to ship a lot of film to Karhachiba. I'll pick it up on the return trip if we're successful and use it on a second expedition. Not too much to report really. Give my love to Joan.

Bob

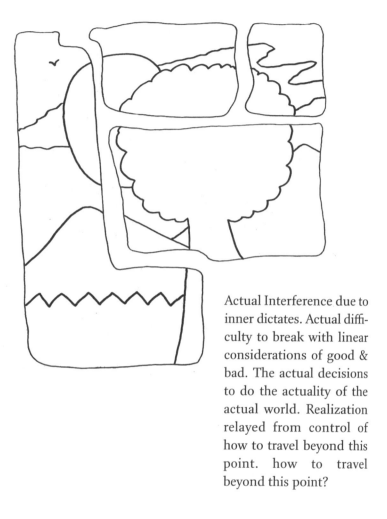

Actual Interference due to inner dictates. Actual difficulty to break with linear considerations of good & bad. The actual decisions to do the actuality of the actual world. Realization relayed from control of how to travel beyond this point. how to travel beyond this point?

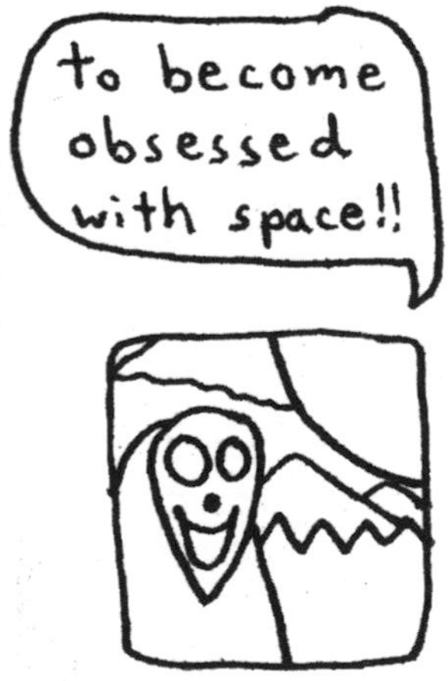
to become obsessed with space!!

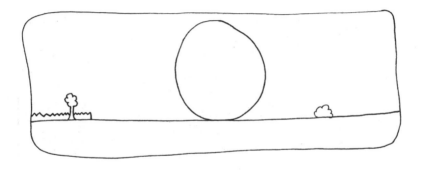

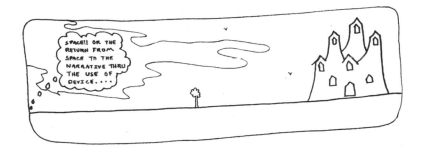

altimeter falling. storm front nearing point of intimate contact. captain. this is your captain speaking. all reference must now be left behind. entering space of opening door to sea. must be realized a literature of contemporary free from chains of past consideration. this is your captain speaking. please abandon all hope of retention of old in ultimate breakthru into new.

forcing her legs apart he shoved his great prick into her moist cunt. she writhed and squirmed beneath him screaming all the time, 'fuck you rory!! and fuck your great dick too! if i get my teeth on it i'll bite it off!!'

speeding into point of intimate exposure. loss of retention due to falling off of windows.

Dear Joan,

No luck at all yet. Had map for some of the time into the mountains but ran into a huge rock field where sliding stone presents constant hazard. Crossing appears impossible. We camped in front of here on the 18th and wandered around yesterday trying to arrive at a solution to the problem. We've decided there is nothing to do but attempt a crossing by foot. Only six of us are going. I'm leaving two men behind in order to increase our food supply. Gave them enough to get back to Karachiba and redistributed the rest among the men. Will give this letter to the two men to mail. We attempt the crossing this afternoon.

'But it's such an intricate situation!' 'My dear to a doctor there is no reality beyond the needs of his patients. We must be beyond the ordinary human weaknesses.'

'Do you get the drift?' I had the drift. A was sleeping with B who was married to C who had life or death control over A and who was also sleeping with D. D's real name was E and she was also sleeping with F. F was a rubbie who'd once been the world famous G and was the former husband of B (she had since changed her name). I knew F from the old days and had even slept with E once or twice myself (a hot piece of tail). oh i had the drift alright. there only remained to tie in the loose ends.

It's great to walk around Paris. The streets are mostly winding, short and narrow. Up Montmartre, the hill of Paris, the streets are very steep and extremely narrow. A few feet from the curb the buildings rise up about 5 to 6 storeys & when looked on from above they appear to be a mass of grey & red with a few little channels criss crossing through them. In Montmartre we have the artist's colony & there you can get your portrait done or can purchase paintings. It's just around the corner from the Church Sacré Coeur.

passing thru and on into inevitable movement going down altimetre falling entering negative phase of possible solution. captain. captain speaking. 'leaving behind now reference daedalus icarus bullshit mouthing motion freeing of ship afterburners to enter probable motion of twentieth century space consideration. style to be left behind in consideration of reproduction of actual states of mind and being. falling. falling. captain. please captain.

she wrapped her tongue around the tip of his throbbing rod and brought it hungrily to her lips, drinking long and avidly as he brought his sperm shuddering into her gullet.

It's been a hazardous journey up to now and can get nothing but worse. The temperature has been icy cold. One of my men, Yaboo Yemen, is suffering from frostbite but it appears to be clearing up. The fever hasn't bothered me much lately. Appears to recur only in warm climates.

significance of late arrivals obvious. childish attempts to draw together into abc sequential meaning previous meandering after halt due to faulty functioning of ships gyroscope.

I knocked on her door. She answered it wearing the sheerest negligée I ever looked thru. 'what's up?' she breathed.

his prick filled her mouth & her eyes closed reverently as she sucked on it with great slurping motions.

'scalpel!!' 'doctor!' 'yes?' 'there's someone to see you. a detective.' 'not now!! this man's life hangs in the balance. these next few moments are crucial'

You would have liked Karachiba. It's one of those market towns you're always raving about. It's not that big a town (only 5,000) and serves mainly as a clearing ground for produce from the surrounding area. It does have one thing I've rarely seen elsewhere in this country. The streets are lined with huge monkey trees under which the merchants have set up their stalls. It adds to the charm.

Just down from the mountain we have Boulevard de Clichy & Boulevard Rochechourt This is a real circus. Here you will find Pigalle, Moulin Rouge, the strip clubs (at least the cheap ones or I should say cheap before you enter; once you get in you pay a hell of a lot on drinks etc. My friends & I tried it but had to pay an enormous sum for drinks so walked out without seeing the girl.) (also lost $2.50 admission) the adventure movie houses, many outdoor stalls selling sandwiches & waffles. (Both very popular in Paris) It's like an arcade.

captain. captain.

When I get back we'll have to take a trip up north to some little fishing village and do some relaxing. It's been a long time since I've had a rest and I know the same is true of you. Will try to write you again sometime but this may not be possible before we reach Markettown.

Bob Calabreth breathed a sigh of relief. 'There,' he said, turning to Cynthia, 'it's in place.' 'Oh Calabreth! such nobility!!' and a tear rolled down Cynthia's cheek.

'What I need to know is where were you on the day in question?' Rory slid his hand under Sophia's negligée and patted her on the ass. 'I was right here copper! right here with the little lady.' Sophia let out a shriek as he goosed her from behind.

I haven't been to the girl market, as I heard a fellow say, but plan to go look anyway. There are many shops in Paris where one can buy wonderful things. Before I leave I will go completely mad and spend much money I think.

space reversal time loop darkness brought forward into present space. Illumination to occur at 0000 hours with birth of possible construct and death of pseudoform. actual overlap of thot space continuum in spheroid linkage now presented for all time as sex food linkage of norm twist. norm dissolve in face of false construct of linked information channels now processed as formal message of nonconstructs. speech. speech. care for the living within you. captain. captain. captain speaking.

'discarding of death forms to be supplanted by matter antimatter overlap to inform the death of certain probable beings as death forms in terms of life surplus threat to predicated police brutality language prison. reference left behind as control element of culture parasites. speaking. speaking.

August 2, 1944

In a valley. We are following a river which I am sure flows thru to Markettown. Steam rising around us. Have seen very little wild life here. Much of the vegetation is of a tropical nature due to the geysers all around us. Yaboo says his grandfather had reported that such a thing existed but no one believed him. He seems amazed at the things he sees. I was aware that it might exist due to many rumours I had heard and old manuscripts I had read. Only Yaboo, Vascil Rakim and myself left. Supplies lasting well.

My french course is coming along. Soon I will be trying to carry on an intelligent conversation in the language. Will go now. Have many others to write still. Also must study. So will tell you for sure what time my train comes in to Toronto. Okay? Love to all. Best wishes Bar. Love Andy

She moved toward me thighs brushing together silkily and pressed her hand against my bulging crotch. 'What's it to you where Rory was Gravestone?' she breathed huskily, fingers played with my pulsing dick through the heavy cloth. 'I've got a job to do!' I panted. Rory smiled indulgently and scratched his balls. 'Who're you putting on Gravestone? You know who I really am and you know who Sophia really is. But what you don't know is that both Sophia and I know who you are. Now what arrangement do you suppose we can come to?'

ATTENTION! ATTENTION! ship under attack by slime pods. jettison reference. jettison all reference. ATTENTION!! ATTENTION! jettison all pseudoform.

'Oh Calabreth!' 'Yes Cynthia?'

Dear Barry:

Have read your letter? over again. Something must have happened there. Got a letter from Dave saying you sent a long one to Neil telling him all sorts of mad things. Well undoubtedly something has happened so plans change again for me. Was going to stay here an extra week but now will leave the continent as planned. One week is nothing in the long run. I've experienced Paris. Another week would only give me a piece (of ass) perhaps if I'm lucky. But that will come eventually, Alors! I leave Amsterdam on the 6th of March. Land in Montreal same day. Will go direct to Winnipeg & stay a day or two & will make it in Vancouver by the 11th or 12th. So old buddy never fear Andy is there. The rest of possibilities are just that. I must talk to you first. But please stay in Vancouver until Sunday the 14th and I will make it. We must have a talk. Also the people back home will or might be probing so be a bit careful. Wish I knew more about situation in Toronto.

> Au revoir

> Andy

August 3, 1944

Resting today. Developed blisters on my feet. Camped beside river today. Slow placid water moving by. Went for swim and got clean for first time since left last way-station. Asked Yaboo to tell me story of his Grandfather's journey. Told me originally his Grandfather had gone part way in but have feeling he must have gone much further. Yaboo has admitted that he did. Says his Grandfather made the journey in search of rumored city of gold. It was over a hundred years ago. Reached this valley in much the same way we did. Followed this river for days eventually reached a point where it disappeared beneath a mountain. Could go no further and reluctantly turned home. On way back caught fever and staggered into way-station babbling deliriously. People took whole story as feverish delusion. When he recovered refused to talk any longer because people were laughing at him. Yaboo says he was never sure whether the story was true or not but now believes it because he sees it wih his own eyes.

She slid my zipper down and deftly pulled my dick out. I was breathing hard. 'Samantha!' I spoke her name. She looked up startled. 'You do know!' she breathed. 'Of course,' I said, fingering the nipple on her right breast. Rory had left the room. 'What good do you think this'll do you?' I asked speculatively, slipping a finger into her moist crotch. 'Who cares?' she asked, letting the negligée fall from her shoulders and mounting me in one swift movement.

'What happened to the detective?' 'He had to leave dearest.' 'Are you happy Cynthia?' 'yes dearest.' 'Graves will live. Have no fear. Now I must go and find Samantha. I must tell her of the operation.'

moving into union of matter. moving into mattering union. ultimate destruction of death speech forms. visionary spheroid thot to dominate in globe construct model of working mind.

Feb 25/65

Dear Barrie:

The telegram reached me alright. Can't quite figure it all out but I suppose that you must be working out something there. I guess you know that several people back home are going to be disappointed but can't be helped I suppose. Look I'll be there on Sunday morning the 7th at about 7:40 AM I've reserved a berth on train 21 (CN – maybe a pool train though) & it leaves Montreal at 11 :00 p.m. I still have to get my tickets for home in Montreal but I will try to leave some time late Monday night. I want to do a bit of shopping etc. Then I'll run over to Winnipeg & make it home by Friday. On Sunday I wish to talk with you.

August 5, 1944

Rested for last two days but now back on hike. Saving supplies by eating plants and bits of wild life we can find. Yaboo authority on plants of his region and I have some knowledge of tropical plants. Vascil good hand with homemade bow and arrow and we are eating well.
'Samantha what is this?
What are you doing?' Calabreth
Hons stood in the doorway face
crimson with surprise. 'The
jig's up' I said, disentangling
my dick from Samantha's (née
Sophia's) canny cunt. 'I've
been looking for you Calabreth'
I said, zipping up my trousers.
'Oh fuck,' said Sophia, 'Rory!
Rory come in here! Why is ev-
eryone just bursting in without
knocking?' Rory came in still
clad in his birthday suit. 'You
stay put,' I said, turning to
make sure Calabreth was still
with us.

        temporary cancellation
of communications due to ac-
tivity in rear of ship. this
is your Captain speaking. ship
now on automatic control until
resolution of inner conflict.
signing off. over and out.

August 8, 1944

The river widens. Vascil climbed
a tree and reports there is no
end to it yet. Yaboo remembered
something else his grandfather

told him. The old man apparently
found part of a shield buried
in the earth near the mouth of
the cave.

If you decide to change your plans again I will be in Paris
until the 3rd of March. Please let me know if you won't be in Toronto
because I want to have time to cancel my reservations.

August 9, 1944

Still the river continues.

Calabreth's eyes widened in surprise. 'Gravestone McHammer! But
you're not supposed to be here!' 'I
stay where the action is baby! I
want you to get that chick Cynthia
in here & get Graves out of his
sick bed and bring him here. I've
got a few things to say to all of
you.' I glanced over at Samantha's
lovely nude body. She ran her
tongue over her lips and stared at
my crotch suggestively. 'later baby!'
& I blew her a kiss.

Well things are
going rather poorly here. I've had
a rotten cold that won't quit. Also
some very bad cold sores in my mouth.
Makes it difficult to eat etc. It's been
bad for a week now & today I'm trying the stay in bed routine. Yester-
day I turned tourist again because it was such a beautiful day. It was
cool but bright and sunny. I went to the top of Notredame & took
pictures like mad. Many gargoyles and english speaking people with
cameras. It was wonderful up there.

August 11, 1944

Rested all today. Vascil and Yaboo are trying to construct a boat. I think the fever is coming back. Have very little of my medicine left. Will have to fight fever out when this is gone.

Lovely setting here. Banks beside river wide and grassy. Trees and bushes all back from edge. Strangely enough no bugs around. Almost total absence of wild life a puzzle. Mountains back about a mile from each side of the river. River curving quite a bit until today but now seems to be headIng almost due south. Weather unchangeable. Very few clouds and sunny most of day. Geysers getting less and less. Almost out of volcanic region I think.

Cynthia wheeled Graves into the room. 'What is this … ' she began and then stopped at the sight of the nude Rory. 'It isn't!' 'You're damned right it is! Been over twenty years but here I am baby. In the flesh!' 'But where have you been!' 'Alright, alright! enough of this chit chat! let's get down to the facts'

The church is a beautiful example of Gothic architecture & it's so old. It goes back to the 1300's. At the time the ancestors of you and me had never even envisioned a continent on the other side of the ocean.

August 13, 1944

Still working on boat. Almost near completion. Tomorrow we continue. We have named this river the Saminka after Yaboo's grandfather.

Had to do something else to equal this so went to Le Bois de Vincennes. Saw the most marvellous zoo, with great stone hills & mountains.

They've tried their hardest to put the animals in their natural surroundings. There's this great wall with bridges etc. for the baboons & the lions are high on a plateau at the base of this towering concrete & stone mountain The cages are built inside a stone hill. It's the kind of thing you wish you had known when you were a kid. I don't like to see them caged up.

August 14, 1944

Now drifting down river. Boat completely waterproof and working very well. Distance from mountains has become less. They are now about three eighths of a mile away on either side. Bushes growing right up to edge of river. Boat only way we could have continued. Am amazed Yaboo's Grandfather got through this stretch. End still not in sight. Supplies holding out well.

Rory had his hand resting casually in Sophia's crotch as I began. 'All of you know I'm Captain of this ship. Where we go is my concern and when you signed on for this trip you weren't guaranteed it'd be a good one. Some of you have travelled with me before and are familiar with my dislike of culture controlled space routes.' 'Cut the crap Gravestone! Who put you onto us?' It was Rory speaking. I snuck a peak at Samantha's gaping labia and continued.

Two nights ago I went to see the amedeus string quartet. Very very good. I'm not a great judge though because it was the first time I had seen such a concert

August 16, 1944

We are travelling through a narrow gorge. Rocks hang above us like half-meeting teeth. Yellow colour of this river water bothers me. We are constantly on our guard now yet what we are afraid of we cannot understand.

'I didn't realize the antimatter universe existed as a parallel to the matter universe of culture value judgement. In the decision to jettison reference I drew you together in an improbable manipulation of set theory. The results are not predictable. Captain's log predicts point of impact has not been reached. We have attempted colevelexistence of matter & antimatter to counteract death level of pseudo-forms.'

I was ready to leave yesterday but I had to change my plans & am here until the end almost.

August 19, 1944

Great eddies of a red sticky substance swirled past our boat. Yaboo claims it is blood but who or what could possibly bleed this much?

'The colonel in his assumption of the name of Rory changed the likelihood of recognition till the end construct. By simple repetition of key phrases the true meaning has been obscured in an attempt to get at other possible layers. Having passed thru the door into his particular sea space time form we are left with no alternative but continuation of search for meaningful utterance beyond a b c trappmg influences.'

August 23, 1944

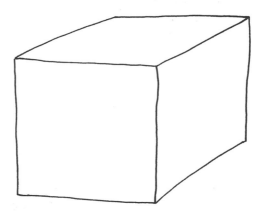

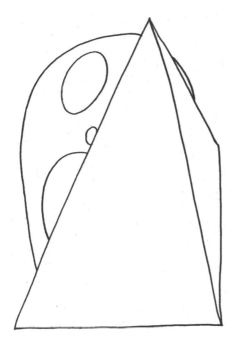

We are travelling thru a broad plain. Thorns cover the shore. I have had a return of the fever and I pray to God it may soon be over. We saw a huge cloud of dust some miles to the west of us and after some time made out the forms of thousands of orange giraffe-like creatures stampeding toward the river. They disappeared before reaching us. The boat is starting to rot. Yaboo says some acid-like sub-stance in the water is causing it.

It is a great town Bar
and you must see it
someday. I found the
book and will bring it
with me. All the best
                    love Andy
p.s. Al Dorn is mar-
rying Diane Haverstock
and they've asked me
to be best man. I feel
pretty happy. They are
great people

August 27, 1944

The smell is overpowering!

August 28, 1944
A huge mountain was seen
off in the distance just as night
fell. May be the one Yaboo's
grandfather mentioned. Camp-
ed for night on this island. Have
feeling I have gone this way before which is of course impossible. Déjà
vu! Fever is getting worse. Yaboo has found some herbs and hopes to
mix medicine to get me through this period.

'Cynthia too in assump-
tion of false name misrepresents case of lost Joan now gone from this
construct and vanished. presence of artificial shaping influence form
of subsequent and previous novels. the implosion has happened already
within laboured breathing orgasm creation of this ship's motions thru
heavy breathing of antimatter universe. this trip to be measured in
terms of my own identity yaboo yemen now lost thru complex of
plastic alteration of matter universe and juxtaposition of unrealities.

August 29, 1944

A boat ran aground on the island just before sunrise. Bakil Sithe lay in
the bottom – dead. eyes turned inwards. face contorted.

'Delineation now virtually impossible. meaning least concern in place of actual working of the mind. purpose to present the history of certain possible heads at this space in time as placed from meaningful communication from earth.'

August 30, 1944

Mountain directly in front of us. It can be no more than 30 miles away. There is no safe place to camp.

'openness a hoped for end of meaning as ultimate a b c concern of vegetable world. door to the sea passed thru and growing. vital organism to exist separate from artificial molding of speech thot continuum.'

August 31, 1944

We have narrowly missed death. Fortunately our boat became stuck on a rock before following the falls over the edge. The water appears to disappear into the mountain a few miles down from the waterfall. We shall go on foot the rest of the way and pray for survival.

'motion to be noted as non-essential. quote from source determines orgasm in the female as contractions of pelvic and perineal muscles felt by penis at point of deepest penetration at end of act. misconstructs of penis as food to be fed on as object of eating noted and determined detail in pseudoform recreation of primal source for this body now occupying new space and time. question of understanding increasing. realized distortion to occupy continual link with own body thru body switch with form now feeding as it were food as it were moving in and out of tight mirror universe of own limitation.'

September 2, 1944

We have donned our parkas because of the extreme cold. The journey down from the top of the waterfall was extremely dangerous and it took the best part of a day to do it. Vascil slipped at one point and nearly crashed to the rocks below. Fortunately he caught up short on a branch. The temperature at the bottom of the waterfall was only slightly above freezing. We spent last night huddled together in blankets and parkas under the shelter of an overhanging rock. This morning hoar frost hung from every tree. We put on the snowshoes we'd bought and set out through the woods. No sign of life anywhere. About lunch time we discovered huge red blotches in the snow. A few miles further on we came across the severed end of a huge vine. It lay along the banks of the river and curled away into the distance. We have misjudged the distance to the mountain. We have gone about 20 miles already and have at least another 30 or 40 miles ahead of us. Vascil appears to be suffering from snow blindness. The temperature has dropped to below zero. The river is completely frozen over.

'details thinning out. obvious exhibition of continued writings of previous journeys thru similar space by the once famous colonel bob de cat now occupying body name rory and one joan batey now occupying body name cynthia. similar occupations of double and triple name space visible as constant in theoretical real earth world. earth now left behind as formal construct of opposition to antimatter matter link-up.'

September 3, 1944

We have reached the mountain. Cliffs rise straight up in front of us. The water forms a pool here and the river appears to end. We are sure it must go underground and through the mountain but we are too tired to do anything but rest today. The temperature must be twenty below now. We will camp in a small cave we have found. Supplies are down to about four months worth and we are on strict rations. There can be no turning back but there is no where to go forward.

'details thinning out. no further delineation possible in face of continued activity of culture parasites reversal attempt of original language tool function now become weapon.'

September 4, 1944

We have investigated this whole stretch of cliffs and can find no way to get out of the valley we are in. Climbing back up the waterfall is out of the question. Where can we go? Vascil's sight is completely gone.

'no further delineation possible ear folding over to avoid sound overlay revealing tonal shift actual message of pseudoform a b c logic. twenty-four year overlap coming to resolution out of history of this head circa twentieth year to heaven flight from this earth and body to be reconstructed of whole manner total orgasm concern for central nervous system completing now in search for spheroid mode.'

September 7, 1944

We have broken a hole in the ice and are going to attempt swimming down and finding where the river drains to. We have wrapped all our supplies in canvas and rubber in order to keep them dry, using the tarpaulins for this purpose. I doubt if we will ever get out of this alive.

'twenty-four year overlap coming to resolution in final flight from pseudoforms into matter / antimatter overlap ultimate destruction creation of total new.'

September 10, 1944

There is no end to the light. The warmth is overwhelming. A strange fur-like fungi covers the walls and floor. Everything we touch is covered in it. It spreads quickly and is already covering our clothing faces and cookingware.

'no further delineation possible. closing now. this is your captain speaking. closing now.
                         Received your letter & poem today. I think I will write Woolston telling him I won't make it to Winnipeg. There are many things I want to talk about with you. I must however make it home Friday the 12th or Saturday at the latest – so I will stay at least

until Tuesday or early Wednesday (depending on the train schedules). I don't know exactly now what I want to say but it's always this way. I know I will have many questions. Things though are the same as ever at the Alliance. I want to ask this girl out but she is surrounded by people all the time & she speaks little english. I lose my courage every time I see her. I was particularly pissed off today because I lost my last chance. It seems that one runs into the same conflicts & inhibitions no matter where he goes. Also my cold is still bad so perhaps this had something to do with it. You know Bar I'm a very funny character. I'm living in fantasies all the time. I've fucked about 10–18 girls in my fantasies & not one in reality. Oh well. A ha! more advice from Andy. I don't feel you should have shocked the hungry pack back home by telling them all. It was too much to take. Although it was necessary to tell them something. I know how they felt back there. It all seems so very mysterious. None of them have seen Toronto or your scene so their imagination takes them away from the reality of your situation. Perhaps your dissertation was a little too vivid. By the way that's a great poem you sent.

 Well back again. A bit more rational now. Went to talk with my American friend in the Pension. Great to know a fellow who can express himself in your own language. But will send a letter to Woolston. Don't really care now if I see Jill. I wrote her 3 letters & no response. Kind of rotten of her I must say. Would like to see the Woolston family again but may get back there this summer. I may take a vacation then after I finish work in August. Would like to see the city in summer. I send this with the love of our friendship.

 Andy

For Jesus Lunatick
(in *Two Novels*)

FOR I pray the Lord JESUS that
cured the LUNATICK to be merciful
to all my brethren and sisters
in these houses. For they work
me with their harping-irons, which
is a barbarous instrument, because
I am more unguarded than the others.

Christopher Smart, 'Jubilate Agno'

the river flowed from the door past his bed   every morning he waded
thru it dusty drops clinging to his socks and legs hours of the day bent
and shoulders hunched to keep our the cold that was already part of
him
        mouth open
                    leaning against the glass staring down at the back
porch stairs covered with ice or rain dead leaves swept clean the night
before unpainted wood gleaming frost in sun returning to or going
from having slept there or somewhere the night before the mirror
above the desk sliding thru murky waters toward the chair fingers
raised and studying them closed against the eye red thot what did he
think in these heads in these united states of consciousness morning
bright against his hand over it fingers warm filtering up from lips
smokey light dust nothing caught long enough to become anything
but memory catching the grey filaments of everything falling back
beyond the blind moving down and up entering his eyes and ears nose

tickling the small hairs that grew there large as morning was further across the room or late afternoon feeling lost in the corner by his bed along the alley blurred rim of shadow bricks by sections beyond all others imagined untrue the many and all touched somewhere before this house himself the sun large in his mind as memory was had been held up against as his fingers were clouding over as he reached voices moving faceless into his ears closing the dusty air they stirred holding nothing close to him as if it were his own hollow mornings he was to become fingers moving softly thru thickening windows by his own wish remaining forever covered in deepening memories his own as tho they were him wrapping thru dragging him down deeper and deeper till every breath he took was part of their softening form oozing from his mind into every gesture out the smokey column of light moving his fear faces not known would be the same passage of time over the few he loved or dreaded

            timeless for this one moment the dust settles in useless delicate motions onto the surface of the tiled floor eyes in tensions cautiously thru the falling air of words rumbling from his mind forever held in memory to attempt the ritual movement into the real he did not feel lean back and listen house awake in the next room below him hurrying past his door toward the washroom other rooms somewhere shouting for their combs and toilet paper asleep behind closed doors turning over blankets completely covering them

in the next room Frank's bed was empty

white cherry blossoms drift down over uncut grass rusting bits of machinery by the back corner where the cat wanders sniffing at the black earth

everything he touched and where did he live how had he got there how did it begin

dust falling little clouds rising where where he stepped toes

roller moving jerkily over the bumpy ground stirs the stairs carpeted two years before removed swept that summer or last spring trailing the fingers along the brick up the tarnished brass doorknob in the dark brown door drapery blue velvet flowers one was always walking toward the mirror reflecting the comings and goings

pauses   in the mirror's surface inner hallway up the stairs past his door to Frank's beyond and a window facing the street below the roof overhanging shadows cast in late afternoon sun

old house of sixty years or more maybe less storeys of red brick glass photograph from the back garden before the heavy green leaves that covered its face existed blurred details in the corner windows voices and strange faces

                                        leaving early

now

        barely light streets and rooms within silent as he entered or left them as now or before laughing and talking fool moving up from somewhere inside him where ya goin fool another face and going to get yur brains mashed inside him just desperate to get yur hot little hands on her laughter and giggling yur always giggling aren't you talking fool morning returning from her thru the green leaves that covered the brick doorways gettin yur week of misery and pain and whatcha gonna get for it ey ah you be kissin her ass if she'll only forgive you knowin the way you left it early morning sun shining dark street before moving

                                    the river flowed from the
door past his bed
                    waded thru it coming home going out deeper than
he remembered crossing further down near the chair slippery rug and
falling always the danger sliding one foot two
                                    hall black and without
sound murmuring behind his own closed door
                                    Frank moving around
his room blind clacking
                    downstairs a light gleamed
                                    mewed under the
lighted window scratching its head reflectively haunched against the
crossbar of Frank's bike light thru the curtain meowrr picked up and
stroked it put it down inside the door strangely forlorn light gleaming
fingers of Frank spreading the slats peering back the line of the cat's
gaze along the street toward the parks darkshadowed trees staring at
the ceiling and listening Frank are you listening somewhere there in
the dark creaking stairs rats skittering are you listening to me hear me
are you listening Frank Frank are you groaning of the trees why don't
you just get up now Frank and walk you can so easily Frank the window
and open the blind who's standing no footsteps along standing no
footsteps along the porch into the streetlight glare in your fingers
Frank listening
                    park benches empty fountain cold and a few drops
clinging to his lips
                    Frank are you in there Frank are you what are you
Frank quit fucking around Frank i said and no i mean Frank the plaster
flaking and Frank listen to me please just you listen please Frank

the river flowed from her door toward the wall that was all windows deeper

than in his own room darker angry as he had never seen her tho he had seen her disappearing into his other face laughing it's stupid you fucking bastard using me you're using me struggling desperately to cross the river flowing crazily toward the window hands struggling under his skin don't talk to me you rotten bastard but baby it's just screaming feeling the water grab at his legs and holding her lips moving softly till he felt her soften and respond flowing fear from his tongue into her mouth her fingers flowing crazily into his belly

coming home early side street house up the stairs sun barely risen into his room and sat down clock tick and breathe

three hours later sun risen out the window staring down at the back porch stairs slowly awakening voices and doors opening fingers tighten on the sill cautiously moving cat paws scattered bits of machinery noiseless feet and his breath condensing on the pane empty bed rooms feet moving by toward the washroom stairs at the back going down around into the basement kitchen Frank

drinking a glass of tomato juice and thinking lay on his bed aware of
Phillip in the next room heard him move the draperies aside slow
measured tugging pretending sleep called him only when he Frank
felt like it

       watched the back yard lighten having left her early light
growing house not awake shadows shortening till the light moved up
the wall and into his room

           where are you Frank are you

                    terrified he
hadn't known what to do knowing she sensed the fear that was always
part of him i just wantakillmyself when you come snivelling around
you fucking rotten dirty bastard get out of here just get the hell out of
here smashing the bottle against the bedleg slashing down and blood
could he stop the blood flowing and screaming Frank where are you
Frank i hate you shuddup SHUDDUP river rising over his thighs fear-
ing this time he wouldn't make it crying and screaming in the murky
water never make it into the hell the hall opened off laughing no more
the good times useless to pretend nothing substains but terror moving
from bed to door floundering deeper and deeper

                       watched the light
grow

    house wakening around him rubbing against his leg and purring
till he picked it up and petted it orange fur rubbing against his sweater

hated the sight of him and screamed drunk crying glass cutting the
feet moving to hold her

             voices and noises remembering later she
smiled and kissed him goodbye wrapped in white sheets hair tousled
laughed i'm sorry i must've been drunk

              leaving the house early sun
up three hours past the park bright green budding trees pure water
from the fountain striking the face

        far away

             farther away than ever
words rising up thru his throat his mouth skin indefinite to him far
away inside his head watching his eyes move

            come back for christ's
sake come back and talk to me anything pounding against the chest

idiotic smile you fucking bastard all you ever do the hell out of here and leave me just leave me alone for once quit coming around and begging

held her close hands moving out toward her slowly aware the hesitation bothered her but unable to do it instinctively touch her to him words rising up thru his throat and lips moving over her body responding eyes red and studying his own

face didn't say what it felt tho his eyes told her and she ignored them

only sound in the darkness what was he doing over there imagined his hands on her body and rage filled him fingers tightening on the slats watched the street he'd gone down thinking

all edges to his body gone and his body flowing out and into her fingers entering every opening falling away and skin rubbing in agony flowing from every pore hungering for and he closed and went far away as i can do i can't go far in

stubbornly clinging skin

Frank are you waiting for my return watching the goddamn street you never move Frank never go out come out Frank come out and face me for christ's sake come here Frank i told you i need to know you Frank please

letting his body define her god where am i and skin beating down on her gagging fear flowing into her as he moved over her breasts thighs lips covered with his lips both of them flowing till their bodies became one and they both withdrew absently watching the twisting form on the narrow bed the hall was dusty

Frank sat on the edge of his bed glancing toward the window back at the door to Phil's room closed feet moving around you little bastard cat pushing the door open and padding in mrooww lay back and studied his feet moving hello Frank hi down the hall am i thinking god what am i doing around the corner and down the front stairs door closing along the porch street toward the park lay back and blanked his mind

looking up frightened seeing her coming toward him through the park i'm sorry Phil terrified and distant how are you unsure smile playing his lips up at the trees and down i'm fine who wouldn't be on a day like this hey and she laughed and took hold of his hand fucking bastard pawing at her god no but hold me please for christ's sake hold me it gets so lonely who was he shit she just didn't know what she was doing here please hold me where are you going i can't even find you sometimes lying on top of her and looking up into his eyes wondering don't go i mean do you have to it's early still why did i do those things i mean why did i hold me please phil hold me i love you you know do you love me phil do you you seem so far away phil you fucking bastard think you can come in here and use me for your little thrill and go well piss on you don't go please phil don't go i'm sorry i must've been drunk you know stay a while longer and just talk to me why don't you you're always going to sleep on me just talk to me why don't you do something for christ's sake don't just lie there i feel so fucking frustrated please phil make love to me phil please you bastard c'mon no don't go phil please just stay a little while longer i'm sorry aw shit i said why are you going i'm sorry no don't go what's the point phil please stay just a little while longer are you always like this you'll never change and don't smile at me you little prick just get out g'wan get out i never want to see you again and don't bother phoning me or i'll come over and kill you i mean it phil don't go please no don't go stay here tonight with me phil please stay here with me the house was quiet

                    walking in and up the stairs

                                      Frank sat on his bed
listening to him walk out the door wondering what he was doing
sitting here

                the dust in the hallway tickled his nostrils

                                          meowrr and
into the room darting its eyes into the corner skittering where were
you when i needed you purring up against him tongue washing the
bare skin above his sock looked down and smiled hearing phil's foot-
steps along the porch and out

                          the park he imagined her there leaning
over the fountain to drink fearful she was there walking toward him
smiling uncertainly hello and smiling back saying nothing but holding
her hand laughing

                    lay back again cat on his belly noting the spider
webs he'd have to dust down the slats getting grimy again cat you old
pile of fur

              purrr and licking the paws purr yeah yu know i can't even
think straight anymore cat what am i thinking scratching the fur
behind the ear whiskers tickling the skin ey what am i thinking meowrr
onto the sill watching the bird outside with quick glances

                                              i'm sorry
taking her hand and walking slowly

                            settling down at the foot of the
bed stretching what am i doing here cat tell me eyes lidded and sleeping
tell me something what do i care ey why should it bother me listen cat
why should it bother me never listening hearing everything silent
noting the distance to the stair where does the mind go cat

                                          stretched
got up

      i know where he's going cat i know something nothing who's
talking to me now ey who's listening anymore

                              along the hallway have
another glass of tomato juice your health cat and many of em

felt his whole body going as he penetrated her gasping lips rising
excitement inside lost before her plunging in without love the fear as
he felt himself being drawn in knowing he could control it but he
couldn't all connections severed open and eyes studying her face fright-
ened bed moving beneath them spreading through his whole body till
every pore screamed with it weight fall down into his hands and feet
body disappearing into her

                       he watched with vague amusement

the terrified expression in his own eyes through the closed eyelids of hers

had fallen in and did not know how entering her they had both let go into the dark swollen waters murmuring voices of the river moving into his ears never to leave you into your head again and again never to leave you now deeper and deeper never to leave you vague in the swirling light grotesque forms with faces he should've known twisted almost beyond recognition hunchback long scrawny arms moving toward him on the muck bottom sucking feet rose in long loping particles of mud rising with his foot blob flesh rolling along behind shoulders straightening with a flick distorted in smiles skinny with boney fingers barely able to move shrunk face gaunt cheeks smiling smiling never to leave again connections gone in the body of another reached out grabbed him sagging flesh of the blob rolling over him she sat on the edge of the bed end gazed out the window

                                                      dressing
gown loose over her breasts swaying leaning back listening to his feet
moving down the stairs and out the door going home the bastard ah i
don't know stood by the window and looked down waving see you in
the park at nine whispered dark streets echoing click of heels under
the streetlamps and home

                         bath'd be good water running why letting
the water run over her breasts and down soaping her legs and belly
mamma mamma crumpled bed bubbles in the ears and eyes

                                                   you be
thinkin of yur mamma boy again i be telling yu no good to be thinkin
all the time boy i be tellin you boy what thinks gets only trouble but
mamma soaping her crotch again boy yur a small boy ey just a itty
bitty boy can't even speak yur be thinkin too much

                                   rubbing her eyes
saying goodbye as he closed the door quietly down the stairs and out
standing in the window waving and whispering silhouette in the still
dark streets always be thinkin of yur dear mamma boy walking heels
clicking house in the dark side street light off the closed slats of Frank's
room

       soap in her armpits and humming softly blowing the bubbles
up off her fingers

                             breasts swaying beyond his reach laughing and
laughing splashing the water in his eyes crying no good to be thinkin
too much boy teeth grating hurried breath on her thighs don't do you
no good boy i gotta tell you so often gonna have to get tough less you
listen

       lifting the slats and peering out feet on the porch coming home
now you can sleep its senseless peering streetlamp in eyes

                                        ran the water
and removed her dressing gown running her fingers down over her

belly then stepping in letting the warmth wash into her

fool boy i be
tellin you stop up the stairs quiet you listening Frank into the dark
river beyond the door stepping soft to the bed and sitting room slowly
brightening hours of listening Frank fool boy don't you worry none
bout him why you always thinkin bout yur mamma boy

lifted her foot
over the edge to test the water then stepped in

spreading her legs
apart and lifting him splashing between them gazing up frightened
and laughing smile questioning her eyes sounds from her lips

took off
her gown and turned off the taps running her fingers down over her
breasts and belly

just a wee lad boy yur such a wee lad ain't gettin you
nowhere you got nothin to give nohow where you gonna give it boy
what you gonna give her

stepping in hands on the edge and letting
her body slide slowly into the warm water

feet slipping on the wet rug
chair to cling to river around his ankles the bed and grasping

closed
the slats unable to think any longer sleep but i can't what am i doing
what am i clacking of the blind closing

let the water flow between her
toes and over her belly cupping handfuls down her breasts massaging
the nipples head back warm air rising

so much dust in the hall Frank
why aren't you dusting the hall Frank why are you listening Frank are
you listening please

sat on the edge of the bed hearing him go down
the stairs the window waving the park at nine glare from the streetlamp
on his face turning letting the gown fall open dark hairs of her belly
closing the door running the water humming

Frank sat up and moved
to the window

MAY 18

DREAM. I walk into a room. There is a girl lying on her back on the floor naked. She rolls over and her legs fall open and I can see the mound of her pubic hair. There is another girl, blonde, lying on the bed in her kimono. On the floor there is a full-length photograph of a naked woman from the front with her legs open. I seat myself on a stool in the corner and begin to fold up the photograph to put in my notebook. It takes me a long time to fold it because it's so large. The girl on the bed has a little girl with her who goes away now and she turns to me and says 'so that's what you've been doing.' I turn to her and walk over to the bed. I am only a small boy but i feel very sexual and kiss her passionately. It's like she's holding me up to her face in her arms. I'm disgusted. Her lips are too big. I feel like shoving my hand between her legs.

Now I'm by the shore facing a man called James Rich. There is a huge cliff on my right and the sea on my left. It's a windy day and I'm gesturing toward the sea and yelling at him 'why does it always come back to this, to the sea,' END OF DREAM

she lay beside him in the darkness feeling the sense of loss she always
felt fear why was he so distant or was it her how could she get close to
him if only he'd stay inside her if only he'd stay awake a little longer
but no and lying holding the blankets over her breeze from the window
stirring the curtains

                dark narrow bed waiting for the loss that followed
frightened phil please smiling and holding his head and kissing him
lonely darkness inside her don't sleep phil please talk to me for a while
tell me stories anything dark formless words inside her nameless please
phil and breathe gently smiling don't go way phil

                          branch outside the
window eyes knowing the hate and love she felt for the body beside
her breathing heavy pulled the blankets over lonely skin touching
miles away

           thot what did she think only the loneliness and loss name-
less inside her why am i here futile whispering in the dead ear dead
and i killed him idiot laughing to herself what'd she dreamt then the
soldier who'd come to get her bayonet fixed screaming knife in her
belly bleeding get your fucking hands off me pulling him to her dead
i killed him laughing idiot breath

                pulled the sheets closer around her
thinning glass of the window curtain stirring for warmth hands drag-
ging her skirt off and fingering her breast and belly fuck off kick and
gouged at his eye with her thumb knife digging in hands over his and
moaning heels on the pavement matched the leaves move beyond the
breathing beside her shiver

               oh phil crying and

                    left her gouged face loom-
ing over smile pulling the knife out stagger dead and i killed him idiot
breeze in the dark room beside his body around her as her hand pulled

the hunchback slapped him hard head snapping back uncontrollably
lips twitching smile watched the stunned expression in his eyes trying
to hold him back smashing water filling his mind murmuring blob

beneath him pressing and licking his thighs agony of expectation

where had she gone?

no longer able to make out her pale body in the river's surging current fingers brushing lightly over his skin unable to hold her hunch-back laughing louder and louder they're going to kill me lips growing bigger before his face till his face split open in a scream eyes searching madly in the darkness to make it back to her unable to think words bubbling in his throat caught there exploding thru his eyes blob consuming him bit by bit eating its way thru his belly mouth encircling his ribs toward his heart

gone why

face scream-
ing soundless eyes escaping thin man growing smaller and smaller hunchback towering over him mouth gaping floating away in the darkened water felt her fingers brush his chest and moaning struggle to follow pain as the hunchback hit him

meowrr sniffing the black earth up motion of curtain at the window
padding toward the door here kitty kitty c'mon give you a dish of
mother's milk kitty picked up and petted and put down rough tongue
lapping at the bowl
                        a mother's blood laughed glass in hand
                                                        padding
up the stairs curl in a chair licking the orange cat meowrr oh c'mon
then stroking and petting but i'm on my way upstairs cat why don't
you come with old Frank ey c'mon curling deeper in the chair okay
okay and sleeping
                        eyes open ears back and up noiselessly arching the
whole body stairs pressing against the door and in rubbing against
the legs purr hello cat i thot you were in the garden c'mon behind the
ear purr hello cat i thot purr hunh but i gotta go you know it's almost
nine c'mon you wanta go no and down padding after him out the
door hello Frank along the hall and up on the bed meowrr you again
c'mon then where were you when i needed you ey curled up on his
belly purring what's old Frank up to cat flutter of wings beyond the
window jump onto the sill and watch on the bed again and sleep
                                                        your

health cat and many of em

smashing into his face and hands Frank screaming and hair down please dad stop don't hit her for god's sake dad shuttup Frank and crying the hunchback overriding phil phil bayonet in no dad no please catch in the throat and yur dead scream please dad you fucking slut and his hand coming down on her crying no please no just get yur hands off her blob rolling over him licking and slavering oh god no fool i told yu stop thinkin of her but i no please i can't think of her now you fucking whore fucking drunk dad get your goddamn hands off of her sticking it in twist and blood on her belly screaming what's wrong oh phil and hands striking down on his face opening above him laughing no dad no crying didn't you ever listen boy fool shuttup fool you be never listenin i be tellin yu please for god's sake dad you'll kill her hands bleeding and watching the knife slip in and out the hole in her belly crying please phil hold me please crying oh god dad no not again oh god crying every night please and i told you shuttup no god NO SHUTTUP don't let go phil just hold me please make love to me screaming lips opening lear face above back hunched and sobbing please dad don't hit her again laughing again here cat

      up and purrr can't even think straight cat i'm holding too much back Frank purr Frank how come you never like talk you know oh fuck off man no i mean Frank you just like keep sayin that i mean i thot like you know people were sposed to talk to each other Frank and you never talk Frank holding her back fur scratch and purr

                                           what's to

say

      you know Frank i mean i know so little about you Frank like who you are are you feeling really i mean Frank like you know you never tell me Frank i mean i know some things Frank i mean but Frank curtain blowing car in street Frank you just never seem to be able hardly to say hello any more Frank like you never i mean talk to me Frank

      for christ's sake i'm not obliged to you know

                                     cat in the window purring moving back car rolling and purr here holding her scratch scratch whatta you want from me purr keep coming what do you want from me always asking what do you want from me

                               i mean Frank i mean you know what i mean Frank i mean uhh well Frank look Frank you know uhh please Frank uhh i uhh Frank i uhhh well unhh look i mean Frank uhh

      cat?

dust tickling lying down to sleep perhaps dreaming woke startled jour-
nal down and wrote

MAY 18

afternoon sun the window thinking
park and after walking talking hand and i'm sorry phil i said those
things smiling are you angry phil laugh and no fool you be lyin far
away and smiling no i'm sorry phil shy and pointing look at the cat
phil he laughed and no i'm sorry phil smile hand talking

sun rose thru the leaves and glass shadows tracing hardwood floor sitting up to look at his watch do you have to go smiling yes rolling over kissed her lips and tongue moving in and out lips body sweat sliding his hand over yes laughed and let her fingers run thru his hair i guess i was pretty stupid last night laughed no hell you know it happens i mean everyone gets stupid from time to time far away coldness moving thru smiling i don't know why i do those things i guess i shouldn't drink hey kissed her again crawling out searching the floor for his underwear pants slung over the chair and dressing lay in bed watching him smiling watched his father hit her again and screaming no paw no shuttup and get the fuck out no dad please stop for god's sake dad Frank he'll kill you i don't care dad stop for christ's sake he's only a boy he should know better screaming fists down and

cat arching his back

mouse boy

hmmm or just a bird

for god's sake stop it please dad keep away from her don't go near her dad just get the hell back slut you whore get the fuck back

what're you watching cat can't you catch it cat hmmm can't you catch it holding the sheet up across her will i see you today breasts swaying leaning on one elbow smiling hair over eyes and of course he said i'll meet you in the park around nine arms round his neck and kissed him

lay on his bed and gazed at the desk
                                   ties below the levels he'd existed
on body becoming his falling into her river joining every motion she
made merely his own body entering himself loving no one but himself
hating himself because his body wasn't his tho she had made her body
his alive inside himself blobby mass of her breasts swaying against his
chest choking mamma mamma steam rising up into the air shouting
because he knew nothing was nothing body things passed thru her
body's violence his violent blood flow out and over the raised arteries
screaming himself shouting up at him thru the closed corridors of his
own mind screaming face in her skin inside his body
                                            was it the same

for her

he knew now she was separate from him terrified to erase her wanted her as he knew her edges falling away each time they moved into each other terrifyingly aware of her as he had never been before screaming in her as tho her terror were his as tho they were one convulsion of fear unable to cling to anything flesh falling away into her eager lips

he should have been enjoying the feeling of being inside her quickly within the moist skin knowing only the terror of finding her body without edges hunchback's hand slapping him as he stared in the mirror where she had disappeared utterly inside him nothing to define themselves she moved in terror to meet him hands shy at side searching his face for signs of betrayal always there because he didn't know she existed

smiling

no doors to return or move thru hands falling into her

searching

searching

soon

the voices would stop start Frank please Frank i mean talk to me Frank coming back in don't put these things on me dying away to a murmur you know what i mean the voices dying away to a murmur Frank all i want you to do is talk to me

lay on the bed and watched the shadows grow on the brick wall

Frank not much Frank petting the cat sure phil orange fur on the red spread plaster flaking on the ceiling and the hall Frank could you dust the hall meoww okay okay but don't lay all this stuff on me all the time i'm sorry Frank Frank are you listening

terror dying away hold me phil i'm sorry kissing and moving her tongue into his ear

did you feed the cat Frank

moving her lips over his chest and eyes closed and moaning rolling over and body moving into her gasp

sure phil

he rang the doorbell and waited

                                  stuck her head out the window smiled
and waved told her she looked beautiful looked at him strangely
running his fingers along her shoulder touching the cool drops of
perspiration with his tongue distant this morning

                                        so many loose ends

so many things unsaid

                            walked thru the park looking up at the stars
talking home and took off their clothes and made love the river begin-
ning its slow murmuring in their heads

Journal

for Sheila Watson

she walked out the door into the arms of another life   slowly as in a
dream as in a row of as's likes & stepped off of the curb out of the
window wondering   having grown old in wonder with no one to
wonder of her   of her being   of everything i have ever known she
thot not quite awake & wishing   if i were older   if i were not the
same   walked out of the window into the dark morning saying
goodbye to you love for now & forever goodbye to you then & left
him   walked out & left him   goodbye   & then

once   once upon the piling up of such beginnings she began a differ-
ent life   of her old life we know too much   more really than we
want to know than what is necessary   streets bare of trees   trees
bare of leaves   living bare of anything worth living for she left it
behind left him behind & went away   & her breasts ached as if the
milk were in them still   it wasnt   she went away

                                                someday   someday
i will tell that story to someone   someday therell be someone to tell
it to   there was no one was there   no there was no one   so why
bother to pack the bag then   & she left him sleeping & left to stay
    i am staying by leaving she thot half smiling   always i will be a
memory to him better than i am now living with him & she went
away half smiling or crying & couldnt remember his name   always
after & forever she wondered what his name was & sometimes it didnt
matter & sometimes it did but she was gone & it was one way never to
find him & she never did

                                        surely there is no one living who remembers
their names   she was only young when she left him & the dead
child she did not remember   left him & went away into the past
into her own future presence in the present world   went away as we
were saying went away & came to join us here   always we will recall
that day   always we will remember the time she came in sight on
the dusty road her red dress visible a mile away asking us saying i have
come to stay with you   & of course we welcomed her in   of course
we said to her then you are welcome here & she was & i was only ten
but she was welcome we did welcome her in

                                                oh lady   oh lady lately
i am so full of that memory of you   sick in bed i can dream of
nothing else   sick in bed it is your face i see before me   always
always as it was then   always as it will be   always

                                                today i am so
sure of my own death   today there is a quick image of no image
moment of being no being again   endless cycle   quick bliss of
ignorant darkness knowing

                                we know i cannot survive   we know we
will survive   & lady we remember that day you came amongst us
we remember that time we took you in & what happened then   oh
yes we do remember

1

1

as these things are they are only dreams as i have told foretold the
wish it seems to be made whole as words are extensions of our fears &
longings   lift me up lift me up   oh heaven is in my holding vision
to be all spheres of wisdom handed down the long roads & calling my
name a falling into the screams & strictures of this life   give it up
then   i have given it up   thrown away the rules by which my days
were named   thrown away the names they used to claim me   them
    them   a calling after the fogs that cloud my mind   all language
simply the knowledge of naming simply all it has become   oh once
was a day remember that day you spoke to me & the names were gone
forever i thot as then you did speak saying to me those things you said
without names   i lay in bed sick at heart & longing   i lay in bed &
heard you speaking   you spoke to me without names that day spoke
to me through the fog my mind made   i lay in bed & saw your words
form   i saw your words form in the blue air floated thru the window
& lay there sick at heart   your words formed in the window   i saw
you enter the room to tell me your heart free of naming   dreams of
such freedom   dreams of such roads stretch out thru the window
toward the sea   who walks it   who comes in a cloak with their
mark upon him   who entered that room behind the other & named
me   to be named & oh to have that mark upon you   it is the name
drives you   it is the name draws you   you think it is the sea & you
rise from your bed   you think it is the sea & you leave behind the
one who did not name you   he puts the mark on you & you take it
up   father   father the mark is on me   father you cover my body
in names & longings cover my body with screams & holdings   there
is no sea   it is nothing calls you   father you never wanted this son
    why did you leave your mark upon me   i never wanted this
life   i never wanted your name   father i hate you   father i never
knew you   how can you hate what you do not know   how can you
know what you hate   your hate blinds you   your hate consumes
you   who was my father   he was never my father   i never knew
you   what was your name   i lie in this bed sick at heart because
you named me   i lie in this bed sick with hate   it is the hate fills
me   it is the hate stops me up   i lie in this bed as you enter father

you enter & put your mark upon me   i lie in this bed your mark
upon me & i hate you   you wrap me in your grey cloak   you wrap
me in hate & longing   the sea beckons me i cannot reach it   she
is there   she is that other you stand behind   she speaks to me &
she does not name me   she speaks to me but she does not mark me
     i am free & she speaks to me   i hate you when i sense you near
     i hate you in your grey cloak   father i hate you   father i always
hated you   father you never wanted me   father why was i born
     i never wanted to be born   i never wanted this life   father the
hate kills me   i wanted to kill you for not wanting me   i wanted
to kill you for having me   you never loved me   i do not love myself
for hating you father   father i do not love myself   i am full of hate
father because of you   in hating you i hate myself   in killing you i
kill myself   i want to forgive you father   i cannot forgive you
somewhere forgiveness must be found   somewhere the infinite loving
must be tapped   someone is listening   surely someone is hearing
these words   why am i writing these words   why am i saying these
things i have never said   i am saying these things for someone   is
she someone   she does not name me   surely she will be there
when i come   surely i will rise from the bed to find her   i will rise
from the bed & find the sea   surely she'll be standing there   she'll
be there   i will hold her & she will not name me   he named me
he came along & put his mark upon me   now i am faces & names &
ache with longing   i rise with that mark upon me & step thru the
window   she disappeared when he entered with his grey cloak & his
naming   i walk thru the window along the road under the blue sky
& grey trees   a lonely day   the road is a thin line   i was walking
along it one grey day the blue trees hanging over me   i met a man
upon the road whose cloak was grey   who are you i asked   he
looked thru me without answering   who are you i asked waving up
toward the blue clouds & grey birds   he looked thru me but would
place no name upon himself   why do you try to name me he asked
     you wear a grey cloak i knew a man once wore a grey cloak   he
kicked in the leaves & snow lay in patches along the road   i knew
myself once he said once i did know such a man so long ago i do not
remember tho i know he dressed as i dress yes its true he wore such a
cloak as this   he looked up at the birds hung in the air in clouds   it

is all so grey now he said & looked thru the mark upon my face   you
are named he said someone has come & put the name upon you   yes
i am named i said   i looked back thru the window at my empty bed
      she stood where i had left her when she disappeared   & was this
one who named you dressed as i am   yes   i knew such a man but
he is dead   he is dead since a long time ago   he is not dead i said
i wish to kill him   if i did not wish to kill him he would be dead
i ran my toe thru the blue leaves & grey snow   who are you he asked
& i could not name myself   i am named but i do not know that
name   where were you going i asked   i was walking along this
road to meet you he said   i wanted to meet you & i found this road
      such a lonely day   i rose from my bed put on my cloak & walked
out along this road to meet you   we stood under the trees   i
remember there was a house he said he said maybe there was not a
house   i remember a woman stood at the door   hello i said   she
did not answer   she was dressed in grey like the cloak i wore   hello
i said   she looked across the road toward the hills brushing the hair
back from her face & did not answer   she wore a white apron over
her grey blouse & skirt   i looked into her face & said hello   hello
she said   i did not answer   are you travelling far   there is some-
one i must meet i said   a young man she said   we looked into
each others faces & saw the names there   i know this young man
she said   we looked into each others faces & saw the longing
there   may i come in i asked   she did not answer   i walked past
her into the house   are you coming in i asked   she did not answer
      i looked past her toward the hills   out there is the sea i said i
said i have never seen it   she looked at me   i took her in my arms
& kissed her   i kissed her breasts   i took her in my arms & removed
her grey dress   her breasts were white & tipped with brown   i
covered her body with longing   she removed my grey cloak &
touched me   the longing flowed out of me into her fingertips   i
kissed her breasts i kissed her   i kissed her soft skin   i kissed her
round belly   she ran her fingers down my chest   she ran her
fingers round me   i kissed her legs   i kissed her dark curling
hair   i pressed my face between her legs & kissed her there   she
held my cock & guided me in   we covered each other with long-
ing   who are you i asked   he did not answer   i looked past him

down the road   she lives in a house by the side of the road he said   i
knew such a woman once i said   she wore a red dress   yes he
said   i left her there to meet you   we stood under the trees &
looked both ways   i was walking this way to find you he said   long
before all this began i dreamt i saw you sick in bed   she stood beside
you without naming you   he came thru the door & put his mark
upon you   you lay in your bed dreaming of the sea   who are you i
asked   i am not named he said   i took up the cloak that that man
wore & set out upon this road to find you   he looked thru my marked
face into my eyes   i dreamt i would find you he said   i asked him
who was   it is the mark on you speaks it is the name asks these
questions   i looked out toward the hills   she lives by the side of
this road he said   i turned my back on him & began to walk   i will
find her in this house you left he said handing me his cloak you are
marked with your longing   i turned my back on him   the road
was covered in leaves & snow   you meet another & your longing
fills her   you will meet another & kill her with your longing   i am
full of this longing i thot   i meet another & i place my longing on
her   i place my longing in my voice & say hello   hello she
says   her voice is filled with longing   i place my longing in my
eyes & see her   i see her thru my longing & she is filled with it   i
see her thru my longing & my longing fills her   you will kill her
with longing he said   you are empty from longing & you ask her to
fill you   you ask her to fill you & she has nothing   i will kill her
with my nothing i thot   i turned my back & walked down the
road   he wrapped his cloak around me   she will not be there he
said   the sky was a distant white   i watched his shadow grow
smaller in the distance   i will kill her with this emptiness of long-
ing   his shadow was blue & distant   i have killed her & she is no
longer there i thot   i have killed myself with my longing   she is
gone & i am no longer here   the white clouds drifted over him   i
could kill with this longing emptiness   i wrapped his cloak around
me   i wrapped his grey cloak around me & began to walk   the
road curved beneath my feet   i met a boy digging in the earth   who
are you i asked   he did not answer   who are you i asked   he
wasnt there   i tried to imagine my window   i havent a name he
said   i have no name tho i wish it   how far had i come   i do not

know my name today   once was a day as once was another time my own life began a different course   there was no one   there was only the sea forever & ever as ever my own wish to leave it tho i swam free   oh what a day that was   i was the sea & the sea was in me   do you remember that day i stepped upon the shore   i do not know you   you have simply forgotten he said   the sun was large above the waves   you have forgotten because you do not wish to know   i do not know anymore   i have grown so tired of knowing   now i am full of longing & nothing fills me   now i am full of longing & nothing moves me   i lie on my bed longing   i lie on my bed & let my fingers move   oh heaven is there   surely heaven is there in that lifting   surely i could rise & enter that world knowing heaven was there   nothing is sure   as these things are they are only words one plays with to ones own ends   you are not longing she said   i looked up   you are longing for no one but yourself   the sky was blue   i put on my hat & began to walk   the day was grey   i have become nothing but my own emptiness & longing i thot   i met a boy digging in the sand   he had a sailors hat upon his head   why do you dig in the sand like that i asked   the grey cloak flapped about my knees   such a blue day   the roads wound around us   i did not know where i was that day   i had no name & he sat there playing in the sandy earth   i had no name & he would not tell me   the roads ran out from where we stood   he sat there playing   i had a name once he said   once i had a father & names made sense   once i had a mother to cherish that fathers naming   now nothing makes sense   now nothing has names   he gestured with his hand   i came from the sea he said yes he said yes i did come i did do that thing i came in from the sea   i came from the sea & now i sit here doing nothing   the roads ran away from the circle we stood in   i was lost in my feeling   i am full of longing i thot it seems i am full of memories   when you are lonely & without love you have nothing but memories of those you thot you loved   i have nothing but memories of you i thot   you say her face hung in the air   it didnt   you say her voice spoke in your ear   it didnt   dont you remember   you & the boy stood by the road   he was dressed in blue & a sailors hat   you looked toward the hills & thot about her   she was not there   you wore the cloak the stranger gave you   your fathers mark was on you & you hated him   you hated him & could not speak   the silence had driven you from her   dont you remember   it seems i can think of nothing else   i reached out to touch your breasts   your eyes were full of questions & fear   i ran my fingers over your nipples & you shivered   i ran my fingers over your belly as you touched my cock   i did not know you   i know no soft words to describe these things   i held you in my arms & kissed you   your mouth was full of bruising & long-ing   dont you remember   you had left the stranger far behind you   i dont know how far youd walked   the country changed from flat to hilly   the trees were larger & the sky grew darker   you saw him in the distance   he was just a young boy   the sailors hat sat back upon his head   hello you said   he did not answer   dont you remember   you started to cry & turned away   i asked you what was wrong   your eyes were filled with hurt & naming   i asked you what was wrong   you turned away   i said i was sorry was it something i'd done   your eyes looked past me   i placed a hand on your breast   you did not move   i placed a hand on your breast & pulled you to me   your skin was damp & you trembled   my hand moved in your belly hair   you would not look at me   my hand touched your breast & stayed there   i moved my fingers in between your legs   you looked at me your eyes filled with hurt & naming   dont you recall   he said you did not know his name because you did not wish to remember   the trees grew in a circle there   the roads ran out from where you stood forever   you wanted to continue but it made no sense   you wanted to continue but her memory filled you   the memory filled you & you could not move   the boy asked what road youd come down   you could not remember   the boy asked which road you would take   you did not know   the hole he'd dug was very deep   you looked past him into yourself   i dont remember   it was as if she stood next to me naked   i thot i heard her voice in my ear   i touched her breasts & belly & she shivered   god i was lonely   i longed to take her in my arms & love her   i looked in her eyes & ignored what i saw   i looked in her eyes & my eyes saw nothing   her mouth was so full of pain & hunger   my tongue touched her tongue & we said noth-ing   you didnt   you say you touched her & you didnt   you say

she shivered but the day was hot   you were sweating under your
grey cloak   the boy removed his sailor hat & wiped his brow   there
were just the two of you   it had been a long time since youd left the
stranger   it mightve been a year or a day   the boy wiped his face
& laughed   you really dont remember me do you he asked   no
you said & looked away   i came from the sea   i dont remember
when   you wouldnt look at him   dont you remember   god no
god christ all i could feel was the loneliness   i thot she was there   i
thot i touched her   i never have words   i never can tell you   i
touched her thighs & they parted   i placed my cock between her
legs & she shivered   i could see the terror & chose not to   god i
was lonely   i only wanted to hold her   i only wanted to be in
her   ive never the words   i speak of women & my tongue trem-
bles   i speak of women & my speech slurs   there are no lovely
words to praise them with   ive only the cold words & cant
speak   god i am lonely for women   i touch their breasts & shiver
    i touch their bodies & im damp with sweat   i placed my cock
between her legs & wept   you didnt   you say you wept but you
didnt   the boy asked you if you ever cried   no you said   i do he
said sometimes   he asked you why you never cried   you would
not answer   are you ever happy he asked   you would not answer
    sometimes im happy   sometimes i wake up & gaze thru the
window beyond my bed   the sky is blue   i feel joy inside me but i
cant express it   i feel joy & yet i am not joyous   sometimes im
joyous   sometimes i wake up to blue skies full of joy & am joyous   i
put on my blue suit & sailor hat & go out   you asked him where he
lived   he told you he lived by the side of the road a little further
on   you asked him which road   he would not answer   dont you
remember   no   perhaps he was there   i dont recall   i thot i
shoved my cock inside her   i thot i thrust it in   she moaned &
shivered   her whole body shuddered as i thrust it in   i held her in
my arms my cock thrust deep in her   her body was damp & trem-
bling   our bellies stuck together   god i get hungry for
softness   these words lack softness   you used no words then   you
would not speak to him   he spoke of the days he walked from his
bed into the world   he spoke of those days & his face lit with joy   he
was just a boy   youd known him for a day or a week or two   he

spoke to you & you did not answer   i was not aware of him   she
stood before me naked   i shoved my cock in her   i dont remember
the boy   you say he wore a sailor hat   you say his suit was
blue   you say he dug a hole in the ground   i dont remember   the
road was long   youd been walking for months it seemed there was
some house you were trying to get to   the stranger had told you
where to find it   there was that night that one night before you met
the boy   my feet were sore   i sat down on a rock to rest them   a
girl approached me from the woods   her breasts were small & she
trembled   no   there was no boy   i remember she put a hand
over her breasts & smiled   no   i dont remember   youd been on
the road for a long time before you met him   it mightve been a
month or a week since youd found the house   the windows were
shuttered   you knocked & got no answer   the door was
barred   you stood by the side of the road lost in your longing   your
fathers mark was on you & she was not there   the house was empty
& you screamed & shouted but she did not come   she came   she
stepped out of the wood & smiled   i read her eyes & ignored
them   god i was lonely   i only wanted to hold her   i only wanted
to touch her skin   i touch women & my hand trembles   i kiss
their bellies & am sick with sweat   you are only lonely he said   you
lack love he said   i looked into his eyes & knew it was true   i
looked into his eyes & knew my love was nothing   i gave because i
did not want to be given to   i gave to hold my longing in   by
giving i denied my loneliness   my loneliness denies my loving   you
are perfect in your loneliness he said   you look in your mirrors full
of self-love & loathing   only you know your nothingness   only
you know your fear   i looked into his eyes   he seemed so
young   you are only a boy i said   i said i know ive met you
before   you have never met me he said   once he said once you
knew me   he touched his scarred nose   the sailors hat sat back
upon his head   you wear a grey cloak he said i knew a man once
wore a grey cloak   it was such a blue day   he poked his shovel in
the dry earth & began to dig   no i said no i am not that man   i
met him once i said   the man i knew wore a grey cloak like you he
said   i turned away & began to walk   his voice was very distant   i
turned & looked back at the spot where he had been   i drew the

grey cloak around my shoulders & began to walk   i was cold & trem-
bling   the moon rose over the trees   i am sick of this i thot   i
meet people but it is all for nothing   i meet people & say goodbye
knowing nothing   i lay down the cloak wrapped tight around me
      the trees formed a circle where i lay asleep   he raised his head &
looked at me   who are you he asked i do not know who you are   i
am named i said   can you not see the mark   yes you are marked
he said   i felt the sweat form on my body   i let the grey cloak fall
open   who understands this i thot   i met a woman once who
understood me   she reached out her hand & touched me   the
longing was gone   i was no longer full of the longing when she
touched me   no one understands what is least of all myself   i do
not understand   i looked up thru the trees at the moon   i do not
understand what has made me most myself i thot   this selfs as
known as these words i write if less familiar   oh it is not for nothing
      no it is not all pain   sometimes the day opens & i flower   some-
times the day opens & i move with freedom thru the tall blue of
it   all these words are only nothing   all these words are only sounds
      i dance with the sounds   i sing with the sounds   the sound is
all the meaning that there is   the sound is the loving   the sound
is the longing   oh god i am so full of sound   i open my mouth &
sound escapes   i open my mouth to let the sound escape   my
body fills with it   i vibrate with the sound   i hate the words   the
words destroy the sounds with useless meanings   the meanings pile
up & the sound is lost   i scream with the sound   i live in the
sound   the sound flows around me i am lost in it   oh surely this is
knowing to live & breathe & celebrate the sound   all heaven is sound
      i am caught in the sound   father you named me but gave me no
sound   it was a flat lifeless thing this naming   now i dream i walk
by the sea & the sea is sound   the waves wash over me & the waves
are sound   oh these words are useless   i swim in the sound & the
sound surrounds me   i swallow the sound   i scream the sound
the sound is me & the sound surrounds   ah i remember   christ i
remember   i lie here in this circle of trees my heart heavy with
remembering   in the sound my heart is light   in the midst of the
sound the hope is endless   i was just a young boy   i remember it
well   i sat where the roads came together in a circle beyond the

great woods   i sat digging holes in the earth listening to the sound
     a man approached me from the long roads   he wore a grey cloak
& his eyes were troubled   i spoke to him but he did not hear me   i
spoke to him but he looked away   i remember the sun was shining
     hello i said   he did not answer   the air was still around him   i
remember i listened but he made no sound   who are you i asked i
do not know you   the sky was blue & i lay back in the tall green
grass watching him   he spoke of nothing but his eyes screamed
such perfect loneliness i thot   i thot he has surrounded himself with
loneliness & now he walks thru the world encased in that hunger he
cannot escape from   i grabbed his grey cloak & tugged at it   who
are you i shouted   he made no answer   the clouds floated white
above us   far away i saw the line of trees   who are you i shouted
tugging at his cloak   his eyes were troubled & locked in their lone-
liness   who are you i shouted hitting him with my shovel   the
shovel banged uselessly against his chest   he walked past me where
i sat digging in the earth   hello i said   he did not turn
around   hello i said would you like to rest here   i watched him
disappearing in the distance toward the wood   i lay back in the grass
& watched the clouds blow over   oh i remember   christ i remem-
ber   jesus how could i ever forget   i live with the fucking thing   i
carry the fucking memories like a wound across my throat   jesus i'll
never forget the fucker   he stood there with his blank eyes looking
thru me   fuck off i shouted   i smashed the shovel against his
face   i watched the wound grow where his nose had been   cock-
sucking motherfucker just get the fuck out of here   i screamed &
kicked at him   fuck off fuck off   he held his hands up to catch the
blood & backed away   cocksucker i screamed dirty fucking cock-
sucker   get away from me   i dont want your fucking nothing-
ness   get away motherfucker   get away   the ground was spotted
with blood   god i remember   christ i can never forget   he ran
screaming down the road   i remember the sound possessed
him   his body shook as he ran & he held his face with his hands   i
remember the gaping hole below his eyes where i'd smashed his nose
in   get away motherfucker get away   i buried my face in the grass
& sobbed   i remember the wind was high   i stood up quietly   i
couldnt see him anymore   i took the earth & rubbed it over my

face   i took the earth in my hands & ate it   i let my tongue lick the hole i'd dug   i licked the shovel clean with my tongue   oh i remember   christ i remember   are you happy i whispered   nothing answered   are you happy in your loneliness   oh i get hungry for sound   i brush my fingers over the soft flesh of her body & feel the sound thats in her   oh to be in that sound   in the heart of the sound there is peace   in the heat of the sound there is happiness
    christ i get lonely in this stillness   i sit here at this desk surrounded by the stillness & death of this city   the streets seem so empty of sound   he stood up   the trees grew close around him
    another calls my name & i rise   somewhere someone writes my history & i am named   i hate you for that naming   i hate what you do   i am left with no place to run to no place to rest   its useless   if only you stopped writing i could sit down & think   but you did do it   yes i did do it   yes i did smash his face in   the stupid cocksucker was asking for it   i was only ten you know   oh i mightve been younger   i sat in the sand digging as he approached
    hello i said hello its a lovely day   i remember he said nothing   i remember the air was still around him   oh i was hungry for sound   all i wanted was one hello   all i wanted was that one sound   he said nothing   the longing sprang up in my throat & choked me   yes i remember   oh god i remember   i carry the longing for that sound everywhere   i carry the longing for that sound & grow weak   yes i am lonely i am   i reach out but my hands stay still   i reach out & smile indifferently   hello i say hello how are you   no one answers   i close the sounds down around me & draw inside   i close the sounds down & make the longing me   ah it is all so perfect   yes it is a perfect thing   i carry the longing but the longings me   i put the longing inside me & say nothing   people say hello & i do not answer   hello they say hello how are you   the stillness is perfect   the silence is a perfect thing   no sound comes to disturb it   their lips move but i do not hear them   their lips move but my lips are still   it could all be so perfect   it could all be such a perfect perfect thing   once was a day remember that day that one day i knew the silence didnt work   hello she said & my lips trembled   hello she said & the silence broke   he looked at her frightened   who are you he asked who are you i did not know you

were here you came so suddenly thru the trees there   no she said
no   hello he said   she looked at him strangely   i have been walk-
ing a long time he said looking at her long hair her red dress   i lay
down in this wood & fell asleep   your face she said your face you
have cut yourself   no   no it is nothing   she ran her fingers over
the crushed bones of his nose   i am named i said i carry the mark
wherever i go   wherever i go the mark is on me   what is this
naming she asked who does this   i looked in her eyes & remem-
bered   i looked in her eyes & saw myself there   it had all been so
perfect   it had all been such a perfect perfect thing   christ but the
silence had been perfect   now i was filled with names   now i was
numb with naming   i am no longer perfect i said   she looked at
me strangely   i said to her i said i am no longer perfect cant you see
it dont you know it you do know it dont you you know i am no longer
perfect   i have broken that perfect silence i said   she smiled &
said nothing   i was perfect in my silence i thot god but i was perfect
till you came   he looked at her strangely   yes i know you she said
i have seen you so many times   what do you know he said   i know
your silences she said   i took his hand   touch me i said   he trem-
bled   touch my breasts i said   he did not touch them   take my
nipples between your teeth i said   he let his fingers graze my belly
hair   i held them there   he let his fingers enter me   i dont know
your name i said   she smiled   i let my lips graze her belly
hair   she held them there   oh how i longed for the silences   you
are screaming i said   you say nothing but your screaming   i pressed
my face between her thighs   kiss me there i said   he kissed me   i
felt his tongue in my cunt   kiss me there i said   he kissed
me   god how i kissed her   she held my cock in her hands   come
inside me she said guiding me in   god i remember   christ i remem-
ber   oh that was the day   that was the day this perfection
ended   it had been so long   so very very long   of course i remem-
ber   i do remember   there is no doubt i remember   yes i know
you she said   he took the grey cloak & wrapped it round her   my
hand was on his cock   he looked so frightened   i love you i said
guiding him inside me   i said i love you and held him inside me   he
was so much loneliness   he was so much distance   i looked thru
his eyes into the sky   my breasts were full of him   my belly sang

with him   i love you i said i love you   he looked past me into the grass   i said i do love you & held him to me   he came inside me   he came & filled me with his loneliness   his loneliness filled me & i lay back weeping   i love you i said   he filled me with his loneliness & naming   i know you i said   once was a time i knew you   once was a time i stood in the door of my house   you came along the road & saw me   hello you said   i said nothing   you said something again   i said what i said   you entered in   i looked past you toward the mountains & the sea   you led me back inside & we made love   oh i remember   i surely do remember   now i carry you with me wherever i go   now wherever i go i feel you inside me   i love you i said   his nose was broken   i do love you i did say   i did say that you know   he didnt hear me   he lay on top of me filling me with his breathing   i love you   i ran my fingers down his back & kissed him   i do love you   i lay on my back in the grass watching the clouds blow past   he lay on top of me his cock inside me   i do remember that day   as it is these are only dreams i have foretold the wish of to be made whole as it was that day he lay inside me dreaming   he lay his loneliness inside me & dreamed   do you remember it as it was   i remember it   do you know i cried   i know you cried   he lay on top of me dreaming   he looked so frightened   you have hurt yourself i said touching his broken face   no it is nothing he said   i lay there wishing his cock inside me   you are lost in your loneliness i said   he lay on top of me his cock inside me   you are lost in your lovelessness   i hold you in me but you feel nothing   god he seemed hungry   christ he seemed hungry in his silence   i took off his sailor hat   i love you i said   i took off his grey cloak & his name   i do love you i said   he lay on top of me his cock inside me   i do love you   i wiped his fingers   i wiped the blood from his face   yes i love you i said   he lay inside me   i love you i do love you i said   he lay inside me my cock inside me   i do love we i said   we lay inside me our cock inside me   we do love we we said yes we do love we   we watched the clouds blow over   we lay inside us lonely   we touched our broken face   we picked up our tiny shovel   we licked it clean   we placed our face between our thighs   we love us we said lonely we love us   such a blue day   the road stretched out forever from the window where we lay sleeping

2

nothing is ever the same is ever so different again as that one moment
you awake alone   certainly it is frightening to awake alone
certainly it is different to awake alone aware now you are the same as
when you awoke alone before you awoke not alone   certainly it is
frighteningly different   certainly you are aware looking thru the
square window at the blue you are aware how blue the sky is you are
aware   yes you are aware of this as certainly you are aware somewhere
something is becoming someone   somehow you are aware   today
awaking alone you are aware only of aloneness separate as that is from
all other feeling yes of this & this only you are aware   alone not
because or for some thing or one or reason being as that is forced
upon you aware you are yourself only lonely in your only awareness
     thus the finger is drawn slowly over the taut nipple the belly cock
leg staring from the bed out the window there is only blue   nothing
more   only the lonely blue you cannot rest in   only that blue
alone that leaves you lonely   so there is a morning you rise from
your bed alone   walk out the door thru the hall the house   there
is so much detail you do not note   so many things i could lose myself
in   walk by a window & we part ways   you continue down the
hall   my eye moves out the window   fields   snow   a man in a
car that will not start   his face is red   you do not know him
no   he is a stranger alone in his car   the starter kicks over   early
morning   the sun moves up the edge of the wood   in the car the
man is rubbing his hands & cursing   thru the windows of the car he
sees the house sees you silhouetted in the glass wishing he was there
instead of where he finds himself alone   you are looking
lonely   your eyes get very vague   god i feel lonely   no it is not
like that   i feel alone   yes i am aware of my aloneness   somedays
i reach out thru the blue washes round me needing people in my
aloneness   i was not always alone   i was always lonely   the
lonely leaves you gasping   the lonely leads you strangely where you
should not go   if you are alone & lonely you do things strangely   if
you are lonely & not alone then the strangely cannot touch you
no   but if you are lonely & alone while being not alone then the
strangely takes over & you cannot escape   oh i have friends   yes i

do have friends   but when i am lonely & not alone sometimes i
make myself alone   sometimes i do not touch my friends   some-
where i leave them all alone   somewhen i return to touch them
surely   surely i do return   surely i do touch them   no not surely
no   hesitantly yes   yes hesitantly at first i do touch them   & you
walk down the hall continue as i stand in the window watching the
man who watches us as he tries to start his car   & you walk slowly
down the hall away from me the swing of your hair the curve of your
hips where the hall curves walking away from me leaving me alone to
stand in the window to wait to watch leaving me alone leaving me yes
alone   & the lonely blue floats in the air outside you   the lonely
blue floats thru the whitening windowpane   & you stand in the
window & watch you do   & she walks down the hall away from
you   & the blue flows in & surrounds you & you stand alone   what
does it mean to be alone   what does it mean to be lone a lonely one
only when that one moment you should be least lonely   she reaches
out & touches you   she does not walk away no but stays in the hall
& touches you   you shrug your shoulders   you want to be alone
you say you want to be a lonely one only it is the moment when she is
trying hardest to touch you   her fingers touch you   it is not
enough you say   her words reach you   it is not enough you
say   so she turns down the hall & walks away & you stay & brood
on being a lonely one   some day you will be alone   some day you
will be truly alone   your eyes will close that final time never to open
again & then you will be a lone one   & youll lie with the other lone
ones & be only as youve always wanted to be only   till then you
spend your days playing at being lonely refusing to accept you are
really a lone one playing at being a lonely one   remember that time
remember   remember that time you ran away   what were you
running from do you remember   i remember remembering it later
how the details blurred   there was someone i hit   someone whose
face i hit   something i hit it with   i remember   i was so young
then   i was so young & something was heavy   i threw it away   i
remember i threw it away   i remember i came back later searching
thru the forest for it   i dont think i found it   i dont remember
     why do we forget   why do we forget these things & later so much
later find ourselves wanting to be a lonely one   why do we forget

then spend our lonely alone times trying to remember   there is so little real forgetting   there is only misplacing or not wanting to recall not wanting to remember   oh i remember   yes i remember   now i remember ive remembered before   this memory of rememberings painful   remembering the remembereds hard   hold me   wont you please hold me   but she cant hear you   she is walking down the hall away from you fingers pressed against the whitening glass you sit in your car dreaming you are far away   why do we dream

why do we dream we are where were not   if you dreamt always this one strange dream what would it be   would you always dream you were where you werent   would you always dream you were lonely   there is one dream thats always dreamt   i am running

there is something i carry   there is someone ive hit   somewhen i throw something somewhere   always i dream this always i wake   once i awoke & was never alone   this morning i awoke alone   she lay beside me breathing   she lay beside me alone

good morning i said   she said nothing   good morning i said she did not speak   the sky was blue   the edges of the window white   we had gone to sleep under the blue coverlet   we had lain for a while & talked   we had made love   when i awoke i was alone

he lay beside me breathing   he lay beside me alone   good morning he said   i did not answer   good morning he said   i did not speak   i gazed at the flowered walls the paper the lamp that had never worked   he ran his fingers over my breasts   he placed his hand between my legs   he moved his fingers inside me   good morning i said   we lay beside each other lonely   good morning we said   we lay inside each other lonely   we touched our cock

we moved our fingers inside us   good morning we said   we moved our cock into us   we moaned   i rose from the bed alone

he touched his fingers to the glass   are you hungry i asked   no he said & his eyes were empty   no he said & his eyes were vague

sometimes at night he is like this   sometimes at night he awakes frightened from a dream   there is terror in his eyes then   then there is loneliness there there is   always in the dream he is running

always there is something he carries   always there is someone hes hit   somewhen he throws something away   always he wakes frightened from this dream as this morning he awoke & stood up

frightened his fingers touching the glass   i reach out to touch him
    he moves away   no he says no   he is looking out the window
i say something to him   he does not hear   i walk down the hall
away from him turning where the wall curves i cannot see him any
more   the hall is empty   i move toward the kitchen knowing he is
staring out the window feeling lonely   knowing he is standing in
the window alone   what do we know about lonely   what do we
know about lone   we know only we are alone   we know only we
play at being lonely   he stands at the window watching while she
moves down the hall alone   & he stands at the window watching
while you sit in your car alone   you do not know him no   no you
do not know him   you sit in your car that will not start conscious of
his eyes watching you   you sit in your car dreaming you are where
you arent   the car wont start   you stick the key in the ignition &
turn it but it will not start   yes you are alone   yes you sit there in
the car wishing it would start & watch the house where the lights
glow   the sky is blue   the sky is a dark blue growing lighter   &
the white clouds the white snow the white windows of the house flow
round you & you remember   you do remember dont you   yes i
remember   & you rub your hands over your face over the scar &
remember   i was young   i mightve been older but i was young
there was a boy   a younger boy   i remember he was digging in the
earth when i found him   how was he dressed   i dont remember
    what did he say   i cant recall   there was something happened
something i said or didnt say   he struck out at me with the shovel   i
ran away   my face was bleeding where he struck me   a girl found
me   later i remember she found me or there is something i cant
recall   what do you remember   you sit in your car & dream   you
no longer care if it ever starts   & he stands in the window & watches
you   & she walks down the hall away from him dreaming she is
someplace else   her hair is long & catches   his face is tight &
strained   we were lonely   oh god we were lonely   his car wont
start   your feet are cold   we were frightened   we ran away   i
stand very still   i can hear him breathing   the tapping of his fingers
on the windowpane   why do i love him   i cannot answer   why
does he love me   he will not say   sometimes in the night i wake &
watch him sleeeping   he is quiet   his face is still   what will you

say to him when he wakes   nothing   what does he say to you
     there is nothing to tell   i touch him in his sleep & he murmurs
i touch him in his sleep & he smiles   i run my fingers over his face
the scarred nose the eyes   i run my fingers down his chest   i hold
his cock & kiss it   i touch his eyes   i touch his lips   i touch his
scarred nose & cheeks   shes like that   she is like that you know
     believing me asleep she watches me   believing me asleep she
lets me know she loves me   i am not lonely when i sleep   when i
sleep i am only dreaming   sometimes i dream im where im not
sometimes i dream im running   sometimes i dream i am here & it
is now & i awake & she is kissing me & we are loving   we hold each
other close   we touch each other with our hands & lips   this morn-
ing i awoke alone   she was beside me smiling   hello she said   i
did not answer   hello she said   i turned away   is it always this
way   are there always dreams we wake from frightened   are there
always days we say nothing or more   surely seeing her walk away i
will turn & say i love you   surely i will turn & say i want you   surely
i will say that   surely   no   i stand in the window & play at being
lonely never wanting to admit i am a lone one   & the man whose
car wont start watches me   his face is scarred like my own   & he
sits in his car & watches me no longer caring that it wont start   all
we are doing is watching each other   we stand in the window &
watch each other   sit in the car without seeing if it starts   oh i get
tired i do   yes i get tired   i do get tired you know watching you
watch each other while she pauses in the kitchen to toast the bread
     while she pauses in the kitchen to fill up the coffee pot & put it on
to perk   yes i get tired   christ i get tired   & some nights like
tonight i awake haunted by dreams of friends lost in their separate
worlds & try to call them try to write down what i feel aware of you
walking out the door & down the street   you are still watching each
other   she is seated at the table   her hand touches her nipples   &
i am tired   i surely do get tired   so full of the feelings you will not
say   so full of your feelings of loneliness   it is simple really   you
are alone because we are all alone   you are lonely because you choose
to be   oh but im tired   yes christ i am tired   she stands up when
the toast is done   stands up when the coffee perks   stands in the
window watching each other & your car will not start & you no longer

care   you no longer care you dont you know   you sit there your
scarred faces blank while i follow her down the hall away from where
you stand   while i stand & follow you down the hall away from him
your scarred face blank   & im putting down my pen & walking out
the door away from you

3

how can i write with nothing in my head no pressure as it were to be
said only the longing to complete something which is once begun
how do i address you who are there somewhere outside me as one day
i must when i can no longer keep these words for my eyes only when
inside myself i am loathe to reveal myself to you   thus i conceive a
history of someone who is not me in a world that does not exist & is
therefore nothing but myself   so let us begin again   you will listen
& i will tell it to you & that is how it is   once was another morning
he awoke & there was no one there or she awoke & there was no one
there it doesnt matter   he awoke or she awoke & she was gone or he
was gone & he or she called their name and they did not answer   he
or she rose from the bed & walked down the hall calling her or his
name & she or he did not answer & he or she sat down at the window
& stared out into the spring morning   perhaps they cry it is not
clear   perhaps they smile to themselves as people sometimes do
when awaking finding her or him gone   perhaps they turn on the
radio or the record player & the music fills up the silence around them
perhaps   perhaps they do these things perhaps   maybe there is a
note on a mantelpiece or table or maybe there isnt   we know there
is some kind of resolution   we know something becomes clear
why   we do not know why   perhaps if we watch them long enough
we know why   we know he or she sits at the window because they
dont know what else to do   they dont know where to go   they
dont know where the other has gone   we do know this   if there is
a note on the table or mantelpiece we know they havent read it we
know this   we do know this   this morning i awoke knowing i must
write this down knowing i could no longer keep silent inside myself
the words must live outside myself   if only i had more time   if
only all i had to do was write   then it would be easier   oh yes it
would be easier to rise & dress leisurely & write this down   this
morning i awoke & knew now i must write this down i must say this
he has left her or she has left him & now i must write this down i
must   he or she is lonely they are   yes they are lonely   you can
see it in their eyes   you can tell it in the way they carry themselves
stiffly thru the hall calling his or her name   let us say it is her   let

us say she is gone and he awakes alone & calls her name & she does not answer   let us say that   is he sad   yes he is sad you can tell by the way he carries himself so stiffly down the hall calling her name   yes you can tell he is sad & you can say that he is & he is so i do   i do say that you know   i do say that & i say it because it is true   oh yes he is sad   you can see that he is sad   you can see he is sad because his shoulders are so stiff & his eyes are so full of nothing   his eyes are so full of nothing they are so full trying not to see what they do see   oh i see it   oh god i see it   there was more than once   there was more than just that one time   & now she is gone & she has left you & you are alone with that memory   yes you are alone & sad with that memory   you are sad without her you are sad tho you never knew her   you slept with her ate with her made love to her never knew her & now she is gone & you are sad & alone with your memory   i must ask you again to remember   i must ask you again if you remember that day you walked along the road going somewhere   i do not remember where you were going i remember only you were walking along the road when you met her   do you remember that meeting   do you remember the moment you met her & how you felt   if you remember why dont you say you remember   if you dont remember why dont you say you dont remember   why do you sit there locked in your sadness saying nothing   i cant say it all for you you know   no i cant say it all for you i cant   at some point it is necessary for you to speak   it is necessary for you to open your mouth & speak   why do you sit there so stiffly staring out the window   you must know that this time she wont come back   no this time she has gone for good   she has wakened in the middle of the night written you a note & left & this time she wont come back   you must know this sitting there staring out the window   you must know that this time she wont come back   & who is that in the car that stops in front of your house   who is that walks up the walk & enters without knocking   who is it   why wont you speak   why do you sit there so stiffly saying nothing   you must speak you know   you must say somthing   soon i will have nothing left to say & then you must begin speaking   when i have nothing left to say you must begin speaking   its coming close now   its coming close to that time when everything ends & i cease

speaking   it is coming very close to that time   it is coming close
to that time when the book ends & writing stops & you must begin
speaking   oh yes it is coming close   & yet you sit there so stiffly
saying nothing   you sit there staring out the window knowing she
has gone for good & you do not even wonder who this is stops his car
in front of your house walks up the walk & enters without knock-
ing   you do not even wonder at this   you are so silent & lacking
in wonder   you sit at the window your shoulders stiff running your
fingers over your scarred nose your chin & you do not even wonder
who this is walks thru the door behind you   you do not even wonder
when he enters the room & calls you by name   you just sit there
you stupid motherfucker   dont you remember me   dont you even
remember who i am   & his dark eyes glare & his knuckles are bruised
& white because he clenches them   oh i remember you   even if
you dont remember me i remember you   your eyes are glazed   your
shoulders shrug so stiffly & indifferently   your eyes are glazed &
you do not wonder at his being there   i do not know what happens
now   i do not remember the things i was afraid would happen   i
only remember my fears of certain things happening   perhaps one
of the things i feared would happen happened   perhaps that is what
happened   perhaps he stands up after sitting down & walks away
perhaps   maybe he pulls out the knife i feared he carried & slashes
you across the cheeks   perhaps the blood runs down your face &
you scream   perhaps he slashes your face over & over again till your
whole face is bleeding & all one can see is the blood & your eyes full
of terror & all one can hear is you screaming & the swishing sound his
blade makes   it excites me to write this   i bite my lips & taste
blood on my tongue   it excites me to write this   perhaps it is
true   perhaps it did happen & perhaps when he stops you are mind-
less with fear & screaming   perhaps this is what happened   i know
it excites me to write this   why wont you speak now   why wont
you say what happened   perhaps that is what angered him   perhaps
it was your not speaking that angered him   why wont you speak   i
become so angry when you wont speak   i can only write so much &
then i must stop writing & you must speak   you must speak you
know you really must   your face is so scarred it is   your face is so
scarred i remember now that that is what happened   i remember

now that he did slash your face   i thot at first i had made it up   i
thot at first it was part of a story i had made up   but your face   i
remember now how your face looked all cut open with the blood
running out & you just standing there your eyes full of terror   i do
remember that   yes i do remember that   i thot at first that i had
made it up but i do remember it   yes i definitely do remember it
now   why dont you talk about it   im sick of talking about it   why
dont you speak   sometimes i dont think i can speak anymore & i
wonder why you dont begin speaking i really do wonder i really cant
say anymore   let us say that that is what happened   let us say she
left him & that that is what happened to him   let us say that   let
us say he left her & this is what happened to her   let us say this   she
awoke one morning & he was not there & she called his name & ran
thru the halls looking for him   he was not there   she ran thru the
halls looking for him & he was not there & she began to cry   she
began to cry & say his name over & over   she began to say his name
over & over & to cry & her shoulders shook & she could not breathe
properly & choked & sobbed as she repeated his name over & over
again crying & crying unable to breathe properly   & she could not
breathe properly & she cried & repeated his name over & over again
slumped in a chair beside the window   & over & over again she ran
thru the halls crying his name & sobbing   & over & over she woke
up crying his name & he was not there   no he was not there   she
awoke & he was not there & she was crying & thinking this time he
has gone for good & he had & she was crying & unable to sleep &
repeating his name over & over again   again & again this is what
happened   she woke up & he was not there & she ran thru the halls
calling his name   again & again this is what happened & again &
again she said to herself this time he was gone for good & he had &
she slumped in the chair in front of the window crying & saying his
name over & over   this is what happened   & finally she stopped
crying & sat there staring out the window   finally this is what
happened she stopped crying & sat there in the chair staring out the
window   finally she stopped crying & stopped staring & stood up &
walked back into the bedroom & began to pack   finally this is what
happened she stopped crying & sitting & staring & got up & began to
pack gathering together those few things that mattered   finally that

is what happened   she packed & dressed & walked out the door &
began to cry but did not look back finally   finally he was gone & she
left crying & did not look back finally   finally that was that he had
left her for good & she packed & left & finally that was that   so let
us say that that is what happened finally   let us say that he left her
& eventually she stopped crying & packed & went away without look-
ing back   let us say that   let us say she left him & he woke alone
& called her name & she did not answer & he walked stiffly thru the
halls & sat stiff-shouldered staring out the window & that of her &
could not move to get her back   let us say that   let us say that the
man with the tattoo on his arm & the knife i feared he carried entered
the house & called your name & you did not answer & the knife
flicked out & slashed across your face   we can stop it here   we
can stop it here if we want   if you dont want me to go any further i
dont have to   all you have to do is say what you want to happen
the skin on your cheek is open where the knife has cut it   the blood
that welled up pauses in midair   your mouth is caught part way
open the scream still in your throat   we can stop here you know
yes we can stop here   but you say nothing   & the blood flows out
& you scream as his knife flashes again & again the skin on your face
slicing apart   you say nothing but you scream   & his knife slashes
again & again & you scream & scream your face intersected with lines
from which blood flows & you are screaming   finally he stops
     finally he stops & puts his knife away & walks out the door into
his car & drives away rubbing the scar on his face & smiling   he is
smiling & driving away finally   finally he is driving away smiling
while you stand in your house screaming   you stand in your house
screaming till finally he is gone & you are no longer screaming your
hands & your face covered in blood & your eyes full of terror but you
are no longer screaming   you are no longer screaming as you stand
in the window watching him without wonder as he drives away   you
are numbed & you do not wonder & finally he drives away   yes that
is what happened   yes that is finally what happened   we have said
that that is what happened & finally we know that & can say it   we
say that & it is so & it is finally over   it is finally over & you stand in
the window as he drives away smiling unaware of you anymore   he
is unaware of you as he drives away smiling   why dont you say some-

thing now   surely there is something you can say   surely there are
some words you can speak   there is so little left for me to write so
little left for me to do or say   please you must speak   i am so
desperate to hear from you   i am so very desperate to hear you speak
       i have been writing this for years now   i have been trying so long
to make sense of it   if only you would speak i could stop writing
i have so little left to say & yet i go on writing because you do not
speak   this morning i awoke desperate to hear from you   i awoke
& began to write listening hoping to hear you speak   you did not
speak   i listened & wrote a long time but you did not speak   it
gets less & less easy to write   it is harder & harder to find anything
to say   if you could speak it would help me   if you could speak i
would know where i stand   even now i want to stop   even now
there is a voice inside me says fuck it im going to stop   you must
speak now   you must speak or soon i will be thru   ill ask you
again to remember   ill ask you again to remember how it was   you
went into the bathroom when he was gone & tried to wash your face
       it still bled a little it did   somehow you stopped it   i dont
remember how   it still did bleed a bit   somehow you stopped it &
went out into the bedroom & began to pack   i must ask you again
to remember   i must ask you again to think about this   this is not
easy you know   it is not easy for me to write these things   you do
not make it easy for me to say these things with your silences   try to
remember   i must ask you again to remember how it was   you
went into the bedroom & began to pack those few things that
mattered   you did not see the note so you never read it   you knew
she was gone & you knew this time it was for good & you packed
those few things that mattered & walked thru the hall that last time &
left   you walked out the door finally & did not look back   you
walked out your face a mass of scars & down the sidewalk & did not
look back   you did not look back as you walked away finally   i
must ask you again to remember   i must ask you again if you can
recall all these things as i have just said them   do you recall them
       we will say that that is what happened because it is & it did   we
will say these things & they are true & that is why we say them   yes
i will say these things & i will repeat them because i say them because
they are true   yes they are true & i am saying them & that is enough

that is enough for now that i say them & they are true that is
enough   it is enough i am asking you to remember now that he left
her & when he was gone & she was finished crying she packed up
those few things that mattered finally & left & did not look back
i am asking you to remember that   she walked down the street away
from the house where they had lived & did not look back   i am
asking you to remember that & if you remember that it is enough

yes it is enough to remember that she walked down the street &
did not look back yes that is enough   & i am asking you now to
remember that she left him & that when the stranger had left & he
had stopped the bleeding he packed up those few things that mattered
& walked out the door & did not look back   i am asking you to
remember that now   if you remember it is enough   he walked
out the door finally without looking back yes that is what he did   he
did do that & she did what she did & it is enough if you remember
that   if you finally remember that that will be enough   & he &
she walked down the street without looking back   & he & she took
hold of each others hands   hello she said hello dont i know you   no
he said no i dont believe so   oh she said   once was a time i knew
a man like you   he wore a grey cloak then he did   oh he said   yes
once was a time i knew such a man   oh   yes once was a time i
remember once i knew a man like you i did   it was a long time
ago   he wore a grey cloak & his eyes were lonely   oh i remember
him well   his hands were soft when he undressed me   his lips
were cool on my breasts   his finger entered me & stayed there   he
kissed me all over i remember   his eyes were so full of lonely   his
eyes were so full of despair   i held his cock inside me yes i held it
there   oh i remember   yes its sweet to remember   yes its very
very clear   & i kissed his cock yes i did   & i kissed his lips
yes   jesus i remember   sweet jesus it is clear   he had a grey cloak
he did i do remember   yes he had a grey cloak & his nose was scarred

it might have been me   i dont think it was me   it couldnt have
been me   years ago i knew a lady who was like you   years ago oh
then when i was only ten no more you came along the road or someone
like you this is part of what i remember yes you came along the road
& we took you in i took you in but i was only ten it couldnt have been
me no you can see that cant you cant you see that it couldnt have

been me   you seem so very much like him   i left him finally i did
he left me   i left yes finally i did i got up in the middle of the night
& left him & when i awoke he was gone   you seem so very much
like him   it all seems very very clear   & he & she walked down the
road & did not look back & held each others hands   you are so like
him   i remember him so well   he was quiet like you are   he was
always quiet   & always i was asking him to speak & he wasnt   oh
yes he was always like that   & always when we lay there his cock
inside me it was clear he was lonely   yes yes oh yes it was clear   you
are quiet like he was   your face is more scarred than his   but yes
oh yes he was always like you are quiet & full of loneliness   i left
him finally i did yes finally he left me   he left me finally i got up in
the middle of the night & left him   oh he was always like you yes he
was always like you are now   finally i left him & when he had gone
i cried for a while then left   i cried for a while when i left but then i
was gone & when he had left me i cried but then i left   he was so
much like you   he was always quiet like you are now   so many
times i asked him to talk & he wouldnt   he seemed so lonely   he
seemed so full of fear   so many times i asked him to talk about it &
he wouldnt   so many times he sat here stiffly full of fear & would
not talk   & he & she walked along the road clear spring day he hold-
ing her hand & saying nothing   you are so very much like him she
said i feel as if weve met before   & he smiled yes he did smile but he
said nothing   yes that is finally what happened & finally happening
it is enough finally   yes finally he smiled & it is enough & that is
what happened finally   he smiled & she smiled & the man whose
car had started & who left finally smiled running his fingers over his
scarred nose over his tattooed arm & smiled & it is enough yes finally
it is enough   & he & she lay down by the side of the road & made
love she repeating over & over again you are so much like him you are
so much like him & we repeat it over & over again & we listen & the
man in the car smiles absently he has already forgotten what happened
yes oh yes it is enough finally   finally then they make love & she
holds him very close his cock inside her saying you are so much like
him you are so much like him & the man in the car smiles   he is
very far away when he smiles   he smiles & forgets already what had
happened as he drives further & further away   finally then there is

only you & her making love & me asking you to remember   finally
then there is only the sound of my voice asking you again to remember
    finally there is only me asking you to speak about it   you must
speak now you know   you really must speak now   i am still so
desperate to hear from you   i am still so desperate to hear you speak
    finally then this is what happens   finally it is all over & i have
nothing more to say   finally then i have nothing left to say & i ask
you to remember & to speak about it   finally i have said everything
i can say   finally then this is it & it is over & now i am stopping
speaking   this is it finally   i am stopping now now it is your turn
to begin speaking   now it is your turn & i am stopping finally &
finally you begin to speak   finally you begin to speak finally that is
what happens & i am listening & you are speaking yes finally you are
speaking   & that is what happens   finally it is over   finally you
begin to speak   finally you do you begin to speak yes to speak & it is
over finally you are speaking yes & it is over it is & you are speaking
you are speaking & it is over yes over & you speak you do you are

2

1

so it began   so it begins   we could give it a place & time   we could give it a landscape you would recognize   once upon a time there was a city on the edge of a northern lake   once upon a time there was another city grew beside it   eventually these two cities became one   that is another story   in a way we have already told it   in a way we have heard ourselves already say its history   once upon a time there were four people none of whom knew each other   they grew up not knowing each other   they lived on the same street not knowing each other   they died not knowing each other   there was a brother & a sister   that was one person   there was a man who hated cats   that was another person   there was a little boy who used to take his toy shovel & dig holes wherever he could   that was another person   there was an old man who was going to die & his daughter   that was the fourth person   we're such a funny lot   we's such a funny thing   we is we are & how far does that take us   far enough to see the form of this history   far enough to see we all of us are born & die not knowing each other   this is a story of four of us   this is a story of four of us not knowing each other & how that affected our living & dying

the brother & the sister were lovers   everybody knew it   everybody talked about it   nobody let on that they knew or talked about it   what is knowing or talking anyway   what is it anyway i say   i do say that most every day   the other morning i awoke & spoke to myself almost loudly only not to wake me not wanting to wake me i whispered just what is knowing or talking anyway   it was a usual morning in most everyway   it was a usual question to be asking myself   so i asked it   so i put it to myself as best i could   what is knowing or talking anyway   maybe they didnt know   maybe they didnt talk because they didnt know   maybe thats it   maybe they didnt know what it was they did   daughter   dad   im dying   im an old man daughter   no dad she said   im an old man who cant get up from bed   oh dad she said   im an old man but i wasnt always   theres no man whos always old dad   when i was younger girl you couldnt keep me out of bed   & he grabbed her   & she

slapped his hand   lightly   im an old man daughter whos almost
dead   & he coughed   she held his head softly to her breast   what-
evers best dad she said   when i was a young man i could dance all
evening daughter i could dance all evening then take your maw to
bed   then you couldnt keep me out of bed   & he coughed & his
head shook &   but i was a young man then   & he kissed her
breasts & she sighed yes dad   dad do you remember   when   last
week or maybe a month ago we were lying here in bed & the cat
yowled & you asked me who it was & i said the cat & you said & i said
him the one that likes them dead   im dying daughter you said   no
i said   he wants me daughter   no dad i said no its the cat he wants
dead   he kills everything i thot writing this down i said   me i can
see the whole thing   me i can see whats happening   he's standing
beyond the window watching them   if she was my sister he said   he
stood beyond the window watching them   if she was my daughter
he said   he sat on the ground digging   if he was my son i thot   if
he was me i said   most days if goes nowhere   most days i stare at
my pen wondering if the if will maybe   if they were my words im
thinking   if it were my speech i said   i was young then   i was
only ten or younger when i played with him   we would sit together
all day digging holes or playing games saying to each other all the
things one says   later he was dead   later he was never living & i
forgot his name   later it was a story never told the same way twice
he became part of   later he was an image or a memory or a feeling
only of anxiety like today sitting in my room i began to write & the
thot came back again the image of him digging no face or name just
that trace of his presence in my mind   later he was a line crept into
a discarded poem   later he was the door opening or a scent in the
air or the way someones fingers moved   later it was too late   then
it was not time   then it was me & him & the talking would
begin   always there was this man who killed things   later he was
not there   then there was the fear that he'd appear   later there
were characters & plots for stories   then there were jokes & whispers
under the porch   later there was hopelessness or a vague expression
in the eyes   skies   blue like today   all night the rain fell   all
night the little boy lay in bed listening   when he fell asleep he dreamt
he would never waken   dead like the birds   like the cat later when

this story ends   like the old man   everything grows out from
here   everything winds in   this is the centre of the story of what
someone set out to say   later he forgets the whole thing   later a
different story begins   at this point the whole story disappears &
then appears again   hello said the little boy i said hello   we looked
at each other over our tiny shovels   hello he said again i said
hello   later he forgets this ever happened   when he picks up his
pen he cannot begin   later he forgets he ever spoke   im going to
dig a hole & go away he said   i said nothing   we'd play like that
all day   we'd dig a hole then fill it in   we'd dig holes & cart the
earth away   all day we'd cart the earth away & build up hills   we
dug down   we covered things in   one night he had a dream   one
night he dreamt he had not awakened   the next day he felt strange
    later after this story ends the old man died & he remembered the
dream   there is nothing more to say about it   it is all clear   later
it was clearer than it was then   he was always frightened he would
never waken   is that clear   is that clear daughter dear   yes dad
    after all he's a good lad   yes thats clear   come here   & they
made love   again   maybe this is the last time she thot thinking
always the same thot she'd think feeling his brow wrinkle with pleasure
she'd think maybe for the last time   the last time   & later   later
what would he be   who would she see to bed then with his slippers
& his cane   this is the sad thing   maybe this is not so sad   come
here daughter said her dad   heres the thing   & she'd giggle singing
a song or two   or she'd cry   why   sing   this is the thing   this
is the point or song   i knew someday he'd be gone the whole game
over   there'd be no one to play with   thered be no holes to dig
    turning the shovel over   look at the thing   what a big bug i
said   our eyes were empty but we giggled   our bones felt hollow
but we laughed   later there would be no laughter   later we would
both be still   only my hand moves   only the words sing   look at
the thing   & it crawled away   look at the bug he sang   the bell
rang   she opened the door   his blue eyes were empty   yes   i
was looking for someone   do i know you she said   no he said im
the man across the road the lane the back fence tense his fingers
clutched the cane the sill will she be the one he thot her red dress
stirred with the wind   its him she said   who   please let me

explain he said looking the other way   he wants to talk to
me   please let me in   should i let him in   & the old man drew
closer & the daughter stood behind him & the man who had rung the
bell sat down frowning   once a long time ago i went walking along
the road a day like this i mustve told you this story
sometime   no   oh   it was a day like this   yes   i was walking
along the road smiling i remember i was younger or older maybe it
happens again i dont remember does this sound familiar to
you   no   i was so much older or younger   i met a lady in a red
dress she'd come from somewhere she was trying to forget i remember
how she said ive forgotten everything & we made love her repeating
over & over i wont remember this i forget i forget do you remember
any of this   no   oh he said   i remember we made love i told her
my name & she forgot as soon as i had told her told her again she did
not remember   no it was not like that she said   i asked her what
she meant   she did not remember what she'd said   later i was the
only memory she had   later i was all she could recall   later she
lied & said she remembered   she did not remember   i was all she
recalled   the old man looked at him   i became then bitter   i
became so much angrier then   yes i killed a cat that she had liked
then   i dont know why he said   sometimes i remember that i
killed it   sometimes i realize im killing them   mostly i cant remem-
ber   she was so sure of herself then   first she could remember
nothing   then it seemed i couldnt speak   she remembered every-
thing & i remembered nothing   i had no memory then she said   it
seemed she said there was nothing to recall   i remember one thing
tho   i remember one thing she has no memory of at all   i remember
one time she has never remembered   we went dancing   one night
we did something different & went dancing   we danced the whole
evening   always at the edge of the room   in the centre someone
else moved   they danced at the centre the whole evening   she
would not look at them   she would not look that way   we danced
around the rim of the crowd   if i led her in toward the centre she
led me away   i dont remember she said   she said to me later i
forget   i sang her a tune the band had played   she did not remem-
ber   always later she forgave   always later she was the image of
forgiveness   then there was only that guilty look her eyes took on &

her repeating she did not remember   once after we made love she
cried   why are you crying i asked   i dont know she said   later
she did not remember crying   there is nothing to cry about she said
smiling & kissed me   i felt forgiven   god help me i felt forgiven
later the whole thing changed   later something went strange inside
me   i sought forgiveness   i wanted her forgiveness   i did things
wrong to be forgiven   always she forgave   always she was there to
grant forgiveness   we danced around the rim   we traced a circle
round the dancing crowd   the band was loud   we whistled along
to the tune they played   i had no thot then of forgiveness   i had
no thot then of wrong   she did not remember the song or the tears
later   later everything seemed strange   later i was the one crying
     later i was the one who sang alone   no she did not remember
no she had never cried   oh i said im sorry please forgive me   oh i
said i guess that i was wrong   i cried   i sang the song   i asked
her to forgive me   she forgave   i asked me to belong to her   i
belonged   we danced together all night long   we had never gone
anywhere before   we took the chance & went out dancing   we
had never danced   all night we danced around the rim   she let
me lead then   if i led her in toward the centre she led me away   his
eyes were crying   his body was still   what does he want daughter
     i dont know she said   she looked toward the window where the
little boy looked in   he had stood there all evening listening   later
he told me what he remembered   later there was a memory of
remembering   later there was an anxious feeling inside & a picking
up the pen a beginning again   is it always the same story a friend
asked   its always the same story a friend said   later there was
dread or a movement of the head back & forth a nodding as i had then
when he told me   later there was breathing too fast & a panicky
feeling   then there was only the thrill of listening   now there is
listening to a memory of listening & saying it again   he frowned
     that day something else had happened   that day something else
came clear   i remember he frowned   someone had passed by
someone was near   i looked toward her puzzled   he didnt say
anything   we sat together playing in the sand or dirt   she walked
by & he looked away   she was going to meet her brother   later
this all became clear   she went & met her brother   hello brother

dear   he kissed her   hello sister dear   she smiled   it had all
been innocent for a while   we were playing down the street   she
went to meet him   it was no longer innocent or sweet or funny   ive
something in my tummy she said smiling   he frowned   ive some-
thing growing inside me   he looked away   its your brother or your
sister   he didnt smile   ive a baby in my belly brother dear   later
this all became clear   we're going to have a child   he did not smile
    he never smiled again   this happened then   later the child was
born dead   later she stopped smiling & began crying   later she
gave the child away   this all happens long after our story ends before
it even has a chance to begin   later she left him   later she went
away   later she put on the red dress he'd bought her & went away   i
remember that day vaguely   i remember that day but it is not clear
    first there was laughter & fear when they first began   she was
twelve & he was ten   those years it was fun   one day they were
kids   & then   he looked away   i bent my shovel in the clay   i
felt the thin tin give the shovel gave way   its broken i said   this is
the way it was he said   i looked in the window at the three of them
    the man was talking   i couldnt hear what he had to say   i
watched his lips move   i caught the sense   the old man looked
puzzled   the daughters face i couldnt see except one time when she
turned & looked at me   what does he want daughter   i dont know
dad   she was all i had   before then she meant nothing to me
    after that she was all i had   when she left me i cried   when she
left me i tried to kill myself   slashed myself my face my hands you
can see the scars can you understand me   no   i dont remember
the day the way it was except she'd left & i was crying trying to kill
myself   it was strange   the whole thing seemed changed or broken
    i was not myself   who are you asked the old man   you know
me i live across the lane upstairs the back porch youve seen me sit
there   surely on a summer evening   no   oh   i sit there often
or lie there watching you & your daughter i see so much i hear so
many things i thot i heard her singing your daughter i mean i thot
perhaps she'd seen her   no   im sorry please forgive me   he cried
    he sang a song   he asked her forgiveness   she forgave   he
looked at me with that same expression on his face   its broken i
said   he looked away   she walked past us where we played   look

at the way the shovel fits   its so thin or fine   she drew an imaginary
line   he grinned   is it a sin   i dont know   dont let papa know
about it tho   & he laughed   holding her close holding him in   is
it a sin   only the final wish of a dying man   dying   in the usual
way   once he was younger & then he grew older   im dying daugh-
ter he used to say & the sun would set behind his head in the usual
way   im dying daughter he used to say & all around him the world
grew up   the world grew up & things died down   things died
down as things grew up   everything is growing & dying
daughter   yes dad   really i mean look out the window now how
everything is either growing or dying   everything is running down
in me daughter   everything is winding up   everyday the blood
flows slower   every day the heart draws closer to stopping
stop   & im dead   stop   your dad is dead daughter dear   & the
dread that was in him   the dreadful dread that was his   to be dead
or almost & conscious of it   no wonder his daughter would sing his
head to sleep by taking him to bed   no hexes or potions   only the
warmth a body is   nothing more   for a father & a daughter to be
fucking is a strange thing   strange the song the head sings to itself
after fucking your father or your daughter   the song it sings is a
dread song of the almost dead   the nearly done you in sing song
longer & longer it goes on   longer & longer till soon you are
shorter & shorter in enjoying the thing   & your life is longer &
longer & then stops short & we say what a short life & it ends & the
sun sets over our heads for the last time   for the very last time the
sun sets & our eyes close & it never gets any darker again   so theyre
open now or they were then   so what does he see   its really such a
sad thing to be fucking your father or your daughter   believe me   as
if the world ended at the door   as if there were no more people than
that   only your brother or your sister & youre fucking them   why
should we believe you   why should you believe them   we're such
a lonely lot   its such a lonely world   our fingers touch each others
faces & amaze us   amaze us that theres someone there   glass is
such a lonely thing   to be touching glass only & gazing in at others
loving is a lonely thing   what do you touch   nothing she said   &
her brother smiled at her   how can i believe them   come here love
he said & she kissed him   such lonely things   such lonely ways

being brings to be fucking your brother or your sister is a lonely thing   is there no one else   & he sings inside him   inside him a song sings he cannot find words for   this is how he sings this   just this painful telling or yelling a whisper in the head   it is all faint now   it is all far away   every night the dancers spin every night the blinds are drawn in the rooms the old man & his daughter & the brother & the sister & the little boy sleep in   every night i pick up my pen   then everything was very clear   later it became fainter & fainter   finally it was a blurring only an image at the corner of the eye   now the image moves into the centre   then the image was very clear   later it all became vaguer & vaguer   later i moved away & the memory became vague   i forgot   before that i did not want to remember   now i remember   now i can never forget again   she led me away   one day i went back there again she led me away saying no dont stay here there is nothing here to be remembered   i did not remember   i forgot again   every night i would go to watch the dancers spin   every night i wondered why i had come back again   one night she was there   we danced together in the centre   i tried to lead her to the rim   she led me back into the centre again   i dug a hole   i dug a hole he lay down in   cover me up he said   i piled the sand over his head   we were only play- ing   it was just a game   every night i pick up my tiny shovel or my pen   i dig away the sand   i hold her hand   we dance around & around in the centre of the room   i cant remember   i forget   i remember ive forgotten   she holds my hand   there is nothing to remember she says   we spin as the band plays   there is nothing to remember   i forgot   he sits on the back porch lost in her memory   there is no one to forgive him   the band plays   i return again & again   no   i stand still   i will not enter   i will not dance   i watch the others as they move   the band plays disjointedly   their bodies seem out of time or tune   i am standing outside their line of vision   no one is listening   the light becomes vague   the scene unclear   i am either standing very near or far away

one day in may the man who hated cats found the little boys cat & shot it   later that day the cat died   in between the little boy dug the cat a grave & listened to the wind sing & sang   all that day he

sang & the old man & his daughter made love & the brother & the
sister made love & the man whod shot the cat sat by himself on his
back porch listening   there is so much to listen for   there is so
much to hear   & he rubbed his muscles where they hurt scratched
at his scars & listened to the boy sing   i have heard enough he
thot   yes that is enough he thot   but the boy sang & the wind
sang & the cat was dead & it was not enough   nothing is ever enough
daughter dear   no dad   nothing is ever enough brother dear   no
love   nothing is ever enough we said   we did   that is what we
said   that is what he sang   nothing is ever enough   so we will
leave them   we who are always them to you   we will leave them
here   when you hear these words the old man is dead   & his
daughter & the brother & the sister are dead   & there is no one now
alive who remembers them   & this is a story of four of them   &
we will say nothing more of most of them dead since that day in may
the cat died   & we are listening to his song   always we are hearing
him sing   does anything make sense   he sings

2

always i am saying i will remember   always there is forgetting & a
glimpse of the truth   always the i says always knowing death is near
    more & more certain things become clear   more & more i begin
like this

            i wish   once a long time ago i said to myself i wish   noth-
ing more   this is where it all gets stored up gets released   i tell
tales   i sing songs   i listen to the wind to what goes on
                                                        each day
begins the same   each day i see a little more of the truth   i go
back again   i stand by the stage where the band had stood   she is
waiting for me   i ask her to dance   she leads me in toward the
centre   she leads us all around the rim   we dance to the tune the
band had played

                the dance hall stood where the roads came together
    we travelled down them somewhere   we were there   she had
tied her hair away from her face   she was graceful   i held her hand
    remember the band the tune   it was too soon   she spoke to
me from somewhere saying there is nothing to remember   i remem-
bered   there was nothing there   i smiled at her   she cried   i
gazed up at the sky laughing & walked away

                                    if we danced i dont
remember   if we danced i wasnt there   i am sick or tired or laugh-
ing all the time   if it was night there was no moon   i thot i remem-
bered sunshine   i smile & look away   she raises her voice   every-
things fine   my daughter brings me the paper   i sit up in bed &
begin   i cannot stand or walk toward the door   she stands in the
doorway her red dress stirring in the wind

                                    i am always forgetting
now   now remembering is easy or hard   i am far afield   he is
like that   i am like him

                i wanted to begin at the beginning   some-
how its all the same or so different it doesnt matter   some days i

cant begin   some days the anxiety is too great i push the pen away
saying not today gazing out the window i want to cry or scream or sit
by myself quietly dreaming   that is not quite true   i dont know
what to do the anxious feeling is too large inside me i try to fix it with
a name the same feeling as today a man brought me my pen & looked
at me i looked away murmuring not today no letting my eyes close
praying

          now i am tired   my eyes close for a while   i'll open them
again   i'll pick up my pen   the anxious feeling will be a little
less   i'll begin

              i wish   often i dont wish at all any more   once i
wished all of the time   now there is wishing from time to
time   soon i will never wish again

                    every morning i begin   some-
times i dont begin at all   not today i say & will not pick up my pen
      my father points his finger at me   he calls me a bad boy   i am
sad or angry or full of joy   i hit the table with my tiny spoon   my
mother brings me the red bib & the pen   i pick up the paper &
begin

              once it was all different   once i danced with ease around the
room   the crowds thinned as we moved watching us   we danced
all night to the same tune   i asked the band to play it again   finally
there was no one left in the room but me & her dancing   i threw
them money & they played   i threw them money till finally there
was no more money & no more band & no more tune   i whistled in
the empty room   we danced around to the tune i whistled   it is
all so strange   it will never be the same

                        every evening i walk down
the road toward the dance hall   every evening i approach the young
boy digging there   his hair is blonde   he wears a sailor cap upon
his head   i ask him who he is   he does not answer   i ask him for
his name   he turns away

                    every night i enter the dance hall   every
night i listen to the band   she is there   she isnt there   i tell her

i love her   i tell her i dont care   every night i try to memorize the
tune   every morning it slips away   i say that but i say it wrong
     every morning it is gone   there is no knowledge of its passing or
sense that i had known it before   every night is the first time   every
night strikes me for the first time   i come walking down the road
whistling   the sky is a constant shade of blue or purple or there are
clouds there a fog has fallen i wander in

                                             once it was all so clear
     once i held her near as we danced across the floor   she had stood
in the doorway watching as i passed her   i walked around the room
listening watching the dancers as they moved   later we danced in
the centre   then i asked her & we danced around the rim

                                                          every
evening i leave my room to walk down the road   every evening he is
there digging in the dry earth   one night she was not there or i met
her earlier   she came walking out of the wood   she slapped me in
the face   i cannot remember this   i think it happened   someone
told me later this is how it was   i could not remember

                                                 once it was
all so clear   every morning i took out my pen & began again   i
would write the story as i remembered it   her dress was red   she
wore a sailors cap upon her head   she took the toy shovel from the
old mans hand & gave it to me   thank you i said thank you   they
said nothing   would you like to walk with me im not going far   she
looked away   the day was hot & still   will you come with me   the
old man took hold of her hand   i walked away

                                             some days it is like
this   some days nothing comes clear   i hold my tiny pen very near
or dig holes in the earth with it   everything seems very far
away   everything seems vague   i think she enters my room   i
think she stands behind me as he names me

                                             every evening i get up
to leave or try to   i cry out to her or whisper her name   she forgives
me   she forgave   i say her name over & over   i write it down
     my fingers cramp i cannot hold the pen   then i couldve written

it easily   then everything was clear   later everything became
vague   now i have forgotten   i want to hold her near   i cant
remember her name

i wish   i wish i could wish & believe it   if
only if made sense   if only i could believe in maybe   probably
maybe will make sense   maybe if will come clear   maybe if i wish
probably will become believable   i'll get up cheerful   i'll step thru
the window onto the road   i'll walk away   i'll meet someone
maybe

once it was too cold   once it was so cold i couldnt leave   i
stayed in the room   i watched the snow   she lay beside me not
speaking   if we talked i dont remember   if we talked it isnt clear
it couldve been winter or summer   she couldve been near me or
far away   i dont remember the day   i dont remember the time
later she was a line i crossed out of a bad poem   later she was
grown away from me   later she left   later she was a memory came
into the mind unbidden   i thot of her face   it smiled   later it
did not smile   this all happened later   some of it happened then
now it is happening again

always i am wishing i could remem-
ber   always i wish & the wish becomes vague   if only she were
here   if only the road would lead there   it leads there   she places
the shovel on the ground & looks at me

every morning i awake fright-
ened   every morning my sister brings me the pen   good morning
love i say   she smiles   good morning love she says   & then

every
morning i feel so anxious   every morning there is a fear   i am
tense or unable to begin   i think of words   they dont make
sense   i write them down then cross them out   i begin again

i
went back   one day i went back   i walked up to the door of the
house & went in   a man was standing there his face blank   i cant
remember what happened then

each day begins the same   every
night ends the same way   i begin by picking up my pen   when
the day ends i am dancing by myself in the middle of the room   i
know the next day will be the same   i'll open my eyes   i'll pick up
my pen   & then

once upon a time this story began differently
once i saw everything with clarity   there was no anxious feeling then
there was me & her & that was all then   later some things became
vague   i tried to make them clear   this made me anxious or angry
i was never sure   now everything begins the same   me picking
up my pen & my daughter bringing me the paper again

some days
things are different or seem that way   i walk past the dance hall into
the town   i see the house where we once lived   i walk up the steps
to go inside   i go away   i go away frowning or laughing or trying
to say goodbye

so often i get up tired   so often there is nothing to
say   sometimes shes here   sometimes we make love   that was all
so long ago   long ago she left   long ago i died   long ago i grew
up & left her behind   she is dead or old   she'll never be back
again   i keep talking   i explain

she was waiting for me at the dance
hall door   i took off my hat as i came in   i bowed & smiled   hello
she said   i took her hand & led her onto the floor   i signalled for
the band to begin   all night we danced   i told her of my life of
where i lived   i told her everything i remembered   she was
quiet   once or twice she smiled   i remember well   it all seems
so clear   i held her very near   we made love   it is all so plain   i
will explain again

there was a time this story began differently
then there was only me & her or we   later there was him then
them   now nothing is clear   when i began first there was no one
now everyone is here   i cry or shout or keep my mouth shut
we are too loud   they are quiet   he lies about his age about his
name   i pick up my pen & begin the explanation

long ago everything
changed   long ago i began a different way   i me or we   him
grey clouds   blue sky   is anything the matter   no   blue road
   grey leaves   please

long ago the whole song was singable   now
there are only words or fragments of a tune   sometimes
at night i dance in my room   awkwardly   alone   i pick up the
pen   the broken tip   my foot slips   i stumble

3

1

maybe there are stories make sense   maybe theres a point you can start from mother where it all ties together the untying oh i do shift plots or points of view stepping in & out of people who are not real to me so involved in apologies & shame because i am not really me

alright mother i start over again i start over again with you just so the head can rest from wandering like i always wanted to mother always wanted to stay there in your arms for hours just to have you comfort me   it was you   you taught me everything   do you remember   youd dress up in your long gown with the purple sash your hair tied back with a ribbon & youd take my hand telling me to dance & we'd dance mommy the two of us would dance all around the room i was no higher than your waist my arms held up to where youd take my hands & lead me   you would never hold me close

you held your arms out holding me away holding me still in the dancing leading in the careful three step three step   you were lovely mommy   i wanted to hold you close to me like i'd seen it done the way men held women & we'd dance you smiling at me repeating one two three one two three & never held me   oh i get sick of blaming

im not blaming you mommy   its all over now isnt it that time is gone forever the music stopped that was never playing we made it up the tunes i mean as we danced me humming the songs i'd learned from the radio you marking the time i am still dancing mother still turning in the circles we described all description part of you as if i wrote from out of you inside you marking the limits of the page of what i say   maybe i say nothing   maybe its simply me saying its over in a different way all the sense i'd known caught up in you caught up in being part of you the heart is broken mommy broken in two & yes its painful mommy yes i miss you & no i can never have you really not the way i wanted you   sometimes i have thot that yes sometimes i have thot i could   i cant mommy   he is gone with his tiny shovel & his sailors hat gone away grown from you as he had to   once you were standing in a room angry scolding me   once you were angry & hit me hard   i wanted to hit you mommy yes i wanted to bite & claw you but i didnt did i   you wouldnt speak to me for days   you would let me help you when you dressed you would ask me saying please zip me up & i felt the skin on your back moist & pale white & the pinks there constantly in my field of vision the whole room the air pink the blades of your shoulders rising out of that white i covered over as my fingers tugged the zipper up closing you in in your whiteness my fingers seeming ugly i'd stare at them for hours wishing them longer imagining them travelling over the surface of your skin touching your shoulders my own hand imagined in the perfect white of your back   & the scarf   i would carry it to you watching you tie it round your neck the bright red or pale blue & i loved you   you were beautiful mommy   all of my life you were beautiful   & now that life is over im starting over writing this story half wishing you were with me alive with the knowledge you cannot be i am giving up the longing the wish for you to hold me & i am writing you at last mommy writing you out of me

2

some days i want to talk to you mommy   some days i am talking to you so clearly   i am lying in bed talking to you but you cant hear me   at the top of the stairs i am talking to you every step of the way youre in the kitchen with the breakfast & you dont hear me   you dont listen mommy when i touch your dress & stroke your skin you dont listen   there is so much i could say   i want to tell you mommy everything that has happened since you went away   you went away mommy now nothings the same   is there any use in telling you this   i have shut all the others out to talk to you   so many days spent shutting the others out & talking to you   its so late at night mommy   ive been out all day avoiding this story avoiding the moment when i'd have to speak   now im speaking   im speaking mommy & you arent listening   so many times i would stand at the foot of the garden calling your name quietly so that you wouldnt hear me   i wanted you to hear me   for so many years i wanted you to hear so badly & i couldnt speak   i'd call your name to myself tired now finally frightened but never stopping always calling quietly at the foot of the garden as the sun went down over the trellis & i looked for my pail & my shovel among the raspberry canes   & i would squat there at the foot of the garden among the canes that edged the cinder alley & i would call to you & you wouldnt hear me & i'd ignore you when you called my name   whats wrong youd say & i'd say nothing   whats wrong youd say & i turned away   all day i'd play by myself digging holes in the sandy soil watching you as you did the washing hung the clothes out to dry arms reaching up the wide collars of your blouse hair bunched in a bun on your head youd reach up pinning the clothes on the line the clothespins held between your teeth or fetched from a pocket in your apron the line creaking as youd reel it out the metal wire rubbing against the rusted wheel the whole length of the yard filled with the clothes the void between the house & the garage between you & me mommy filled with the flapping sheets i'd hide among because i liked the smell of them liked the look of you hanging the clothes up to dry i liked it loved you wanted you mommy but i never called your name   it gets hard to speak   the despair is too close i wake up dreaming of dying as tho the hopelessness were that close so

close that i feel choked by it overwhelmed i forget who i am   & i
walk down the stairs talking to you dancing down the stairs every step
of the way plodding as if the hopelessness were there & palpable to be
waded thru i can hear the orchestra playing & im singing calling your
name as i move down the stairs to where you wait fixing breakfast
fixing none of the things that are really broken & im crying·laughing
walk out the door not bothering to tell you where im going   it gets
harder & harder to tell you   it gets harder & harder to tell who im
speaking to   sometimes i wake from dreams of you wanting to touch
you you arent there i want to run into your room the way i used to too
frightened to go to bed too frightened to enter that emptiness i wanted
you to comfort me to talk to me & you did sometimes i was never sure
lingering in the hall not wanting to go downstairs afraid of what you
or dad would say to me just standing there not moving staring at the
walls my floor theyre all so far away & i want you there to make them
real to me to make the room smaller the light brighter & you werent
there & i wanted to call your name & i didnt & wanted to run to you
& i didnt i didnt i didnt   later there were times i called to you as
later there were times you came times you didnt come or came angry
or depressed as tho you & dad had been fighting you were unhappy
staring down at me your eyes full of tears & i was frightened afraid to
speak to you & you went away   how i wished youd stay   how i
loved the days you did stay as later there were times you took me to
the movies & we sat together times when dad was out of town we
would put our coats on & walk down the street together to the movie
house & watch the double bill & stop at your friends on the way home
for coffee watching while the two of you drank & talked & i would
watch you   ive never stopped watching you mommy ive never
stopped calling your name seated behind the big chair or somewhere
where you couldnt see me watching as you vacuumed the carpet brush-
ing the hair back from your face with the back of your hand washing
the dishes the way the soap clung to your fingers wrists the tiny rings
of bubbles & i'd watch you i'd call your name & you wouldnt hear me
couldnt see me as you reached up to put the glasses away reached up
to put the plates away & i reach up to you & you dont see me   you
dont see me & i stand in the doorway watching & you dont see me   &
i remember you dressing the red dress you wore when i was six & you

called to me asking me to zip you up the white line of your slip above which your skin glowed framed by the two thin strings of silk clung to the outside curve of your shoulders while the radio played sounding sweet & sickly like a music box over & over & i would slide the zipper up over & over dreaming covering you in as you thanked me & i zipped you up & you thanked me & i sang your name sang over & over again & again & you thanked me you thanked me mommy you thanked me & spoke my name   & it is gone mommy all gone like the radio that day i cant remember the tune only faintly like the echo of an orchestra playing & you are dancing somewhere in the corner of a room it is all gone mommy like the red dress you put on you were going to a dance & dad was dressing down the hall putting on his tie his tie clip & his cuff links & you are asking me to zip you in in the red dress you wore especially for him & your hair was beautiful your lips were beautiful the two of you went dancing & left me home & i called your name mommy you werent there & i never thot to call his name he never was there & i gave up calling your names gave up doing anything but dreaming dreaming always i was calling & you came   & once you took me to the sea in the little sailors cap & white shorts i wore playing in the sand with my shovel & my pail you tied the halter on me so i wouldnt run away wouldnt run into the sea & drown tied me to the tree in the front yard when i played at home so i couldnt open the gate wouldnt run into the street couldnt move to where the cars could hit me & i described a circle on the lawn with my awkward stumbling beat a circle with my hands & knees in the sand as i dragged myself round crawling exploring the limits of my keep the sand hot & you lay back & slept mommy in your old red bathing suit the one with the hole in it under your arm & you lay back with your arm over your face as i crawled around you in my sailors hat & couldnt speak couldnt say your name could only cry or scream & didnt wouldnt sat in the sand watching you as i dug holes filled them in & watched you   so many years spent watching you   so many years spent mutely calling your name   so many years of memories that are no use to me anymore emptied of feeling emptied of knowing emptied of anyone who was ever me who loved you who wanted you for his own accepting as he must as i must he can never have you   i can never have you mommy i never did have you wrapped up as you were in your own story your own pain what was it you saw reflected in me as you gazed down your eyes so far away farther away than my arms could ever reach as you led me in the shadow of your longing led me in the careful patterns you had learned   & i learned them well mommy i learned them every step of the way just so i could watch you just so i could await the day when you would finally find me finally see me & you would turn to me then your eyes wide open & your hair come undone & you would open your arms & call to me call to me mommy & speak my name

3

i have said everything i can say having started out so sure i know there are times when words make sense times when all this talking seems necessary it doesnt now   sometimes i go back there to the street where i lived the spot where the dance hall stood back to the room i lay in thru my sickness the place i found the roads spread out from sit & scratch at the earth with my shovel my pen & try to start again that way   it doesnt work   long ago i saw that   long ago i knew that that was no good   now i know im thru with her for good   there is no point in continuing this story   so much seems like coincidence like some novel you dream up in a bad year   goodbye mother goodbye father   goodbye lonely feeling   its becoming vital now that we all quit this   now its becoming vital that we all stop   i must speak to you without her presence   i need to tell you things she wouldnt want me to say   maybe i wont be there when you put this book down   someone will be there   its all so simple really its all so straightahead   it cant end like it always does   once i asked them all to speak to me all of them now im asking you   ive always felt too shy   i never thot youd listen   i still wonder if you'll listen to me   at some point you just have to put the fear aside   at some point we just have to talk   when you read this i want it to be me when you read this i want to be there   its so easy to become maudlin   its so easy to be insincere   everything is here as it happened   i want to be sure youre here saying hello to me   i cant be sure   its unfair really to ask that of you   when you put this book down i wont be there   someone will be there   its so simple isnt it   all one has to do is speak honestly   all you have to do is say what you feel to speak to anyone is so simple   to speak to anyone you just put your book down look them in the eye & tell them what it is exactly that youre feeling

Craft Dinner

for ellie
'a bunch of proses'

Early April

she giggled   WHUMPF he roared & they both broke up little pieces of themselves flying back into the past till they tickled the toes of the sleeping beasties who yawned & squirmed under their skins causing all sorts of licorice stickmeups where least regretted   every word he said was like a finger into her & she squirmed & giggled & rubbed her eyes & said oh me oh my raising the pitch a patch with every poke until his words were like the ferry engines stroke beneath her

THE BIRDS FOLLOWED US TO VICTORIA

FLASH   COUPLE CAUGHT IN RAID ON SECRET LOVENEST twelve fifty a night   he went to the john

i've been looking for you   i don't know why

all kinds of treatmekindlies in his words   every sentence stacked with prepositions

she   giggled   aircraft   carriers   DESTROYERS   he roared   ptsskaboom   everybody   clap clap clap

back in the dark screeches of his mind the blind beasties groping   curling his toenails & bending his knees   smiles wanly   who'd wanta ketchakowout here

bastard beasties burblin in his ear   you with a wife & cuddly gaping & groping this groupeyed girl   why john cannyside i'm surprised at you   he put a finger to his fear

he's so horribly shy & self-conscious   he's perhaps getting over it now   i think it's coz all those years he didn't go anywhere with me   i like him   he's unusual

me   me   hear them talking bout me   hear me talkin bout you bitches   all bitches   batches of bitches

nothing out there but water for miles she giggled

the only one that understands you   is that right john cannyside

the only one that stands under you anymore   you're groping
coz yur grip is slipping

SHUT UP   SHUT UP   she's a wonderful creature   warm
& wonderful   warm & soft & full of wonder

ooh look at that lighthouse there

twenty lousy years as an insurance salesman   I spent a fortune
getting the wife fixed up & she still says no go

no go cuz yur gone john

i was looking for you   i don't know why

face in a toilet   dark beasties crawling up his throat

there's too much gone before   even if she gave him a free hand i
think he had a lot of qualities she didn't even want at all

                                        john
                        inside
            come
                                cannyside

        come inside of me
        mamma's calling to you john
        johnny come with me oh
        johnny come with me

and what if you're found out john   what if you're found
out   they're talking bout you john   they can tell   it's so
obvious   everyone can tell   what if you see a friend of martha's
john   what then

shut up

what then john   hmmm   you're not a young man john canny-
side   she doesn't love you fool   it's a lark   a day in the

deer park with a dying spark

well her father was the type   she would've liked to have met some-
body like him   he wore the pants   definitely

SHUT UP

i'm talking to you john   **I'M TALKING TO YOU**

she's the one the only one   she understands me   soft
      so warm & soft & wonderful

ah poor john cannyside   he's fumbling with his words now
      & she's guiding him in   with experience

FOOT PASSENGERS WILL AWAIT INSTRUCTIONS TO BE GIVEN
IN OUR NEXT ANNOUNCEMENT

everyone else is gone she giggled

martha finds out & you're gone sweet john

everyone else is gone

Gorg

a detective story
for a.a. fair   posthumously

a man walks into a room. there is a corpse on the floor. the man has been shot through the temple the bullet entering at a 45° angle above the eyes & exiting almost thru the top of the skull. the man does not walk out of the room. the corpse stands up & introduces himself. later there will be a party. you will not be invited & feeling hurt go off into a corner to sulk. there is a gun on the window sill. you rig up a pulley which enables you to pull the trigger while pointing the gun between your eyes & holding it with your feet. a man walks in on you. you are lying on the floor dead. you have been shot thru the temple the bullet exiting almost thru the top of your skull. you stand up & introduce yourself. the man lies on the floor & you shoot him between the eyes the bullet piercing his temple & exiting thru his skull into the floor. you rejoin the party. the man asks you to leave since you weren't invited. you notice a stranger in the doorway who pulling out a gun shoots you between the eyes. you introduce each other & lie down. your host is polite but firm & asks you both to leave. at this point a man walks in & introduces himself. you are lying on the floor & cannot see him. your host appears not to know him & the man leaves. the party ends & the room is empty. the man picks up the corpse & exits.

Me & Mona

blue blue blue   brown & green   bluer & bluer   i thot i
blew her up like a balloon   was it fun   she seemed too flighty
to me i couldn't tie her down   he leapt out of the pages at me
    i closed the book   grey   blue grey blue   blue in
blue surrounded by blue with another blue emerging   hello &
goodbye   not again   only blue bluest of blues   blue

§

red   yellow   blue   red   yellow   blue
redyellowblue   green
    un-   no   blue   red   yellow   green
    yellow   red   red   blue   yellowbluered
    yes

un-   no   un-a-   yes   un-   no no
-a-

that   this or that   this but that   or   but
also   and&   but   or this   or that   or
this or that   also

bled   rue   bledrue   no   bled but   yes
    ruebled   yes   rubble   yes

un-   un-un-a-   un-a-bled-abled-rue

that   this also   this   or that this   unabluerue
    red   bled

green   or yellow   yellow   green   yellow   red
    this living

particular conscious mental acts

immediate

plot

blue

oh where

idea of distortion

interesting

almost automatic

a continuation   something like speech likes   lately
        up   down &   down & up   stop

green & something

or something else

both ways a middle beginning ending

Ketchs

i want to start with the light on the floor somehow the point of transi-
tion moving from door to door bed to bed room   the particular
square or pattern different the balls of dust that gather there having
not swept it carefully in such a long time you lean back in the chair
adjust yourself for the listening   this observation is simple then
that you are seated there your ears open your eyes you let the senses
take over if you're careful that discipline allowing a yielding the outer
edges of the body gather it all in the listening points & the learning
      the carpet is red sometimes sometimes the rug is static yielding
to the pressure of feet crossing the floor to join you   sometimes
at night sitting by myself the room adjusting to the pressures of the
day the tangible presence of those who have entered & gone away
again their footsteps what they said recurring my responses body or
action & their laughter tears rage exchange   going to bed or
waking the last traces of sunlight in the room that reminder the world
is bigger the pressure of what is real & outside us i hate to draw the
blinds blinding myself   the chairs are different wood or leather as
the faces of all things change aging i am part of what i move thru air
or water accumulating words books frames of faces & balloons speaking
      later the walls change shape the location of doors & windows
you are still speaking listening all parts of you attent the intent the
same the learning

Cautious Diary

cut two holes for eyes in a brown paper bag & place it over your
head   now read the following piece

forthright actually neither doing & forgetting blessed   here it is
& there it goes   sooner or later or perhaps in between but always
there   there as in here as in there

eventually what emerges then why then how

now there is a little house in which a man sits crying   why are
you crying   i am very sad   it is sad that you are crying
boo hoo hoo   do not make fun of me   i am crying because
your sadness is sad

later there is that or this   his in this   hat in that   his hat
in that makes this   here a bug appears & frightens everyone
eek   don't worry i will kill it for you

i think maybe i like you for that   for what   that what you
just did   what was it that i just did   what was done   who
did what & why   anyway i think i love you for that

can i say something now   certainly   my name is phillip & i
am 26 years old & i am a character in this story you are reading i have
brown hair & brown eyes & i am nicknamed brownie   yesterday
i killed a bug for a friend who was very grateful   i do not like
killing things   it is too bad my friend was grateful

here i am again & there you are again   what else do you have to
say for yourself   well i would like to say that it is certainly a nice
day out & isn't that funny a fly just buzzed past our ears

eating & regretting   i forget what i forgot   you certainly are
forgetful   if i did not have my head tied on i would lose it   here
let me make the knot tighter   not too tight now coz it hurts
        no no don't worry

what did you have for breakfast   nothing   why   i have
given up eating   won't you die   no not really   i'll just

get thinner for a while & then eventually i'll get hungry again & then
i'll eat   have one of these plums they're really great

is that about it   probably   i hope i see you again real soon
     hi

A Marriage

there are maybe two dozen of us gathered together in the basement of the house the home all of us who live there friends & the bride's family
there are maybe two windows open out of four it was a spring day i recall why do the dates escape me the when i remember mostly the room where we were how he looked being a bridegroom & her a bride the two of them the pride he had for her visible in the eyes & outside i can't recall exhaust from the cars maybe each time one pulled into the alley but i know it was march yes march so probably only the one window open slightly if the furnace had been on too long if we all felt too hot no now it becomes clearer to say that we opened the window or windows later that is nearer the truth   we drank vermouth & scotch & beer talked about our private fears or hopes of other things happy to be together as friends to share something the afternoon moving into evening the day blurs together the marriage & the gifts the talk afterwards the blessings & congratulations whatever the situation to come some sense of each other this point in time standing in line briefly or moving about to kiss her to shake his hand   seven years since he & i met working in the library i am remembering that today saying this as i always do each time the two of us end up in the same room how long we have known each other our lives caught up in the same telling those years the details different the outline the same so that there at that moment i was caught up in his past our past together how long i had known her maybe six months at that time he is looking embarrassed tense she glances over at him the minister reading the prayers her mother looking scared or confused & do you & they do & it is done   later the drinking & talk we have all known each other so long our lives woven together somebody sings a tune or thinks of it but cannot remember the words the tune the long afternoon the feeling in the room of the wedding

Lipstick on my Watchband

lounge in the doorway of a crowded room humming & read this
to yourself

la ti da ti da da da ti la le la ti da da da ti la da da la la

Twins – *a history*

woman is born out of woman   there is a womb inside her growing out of which a woman can emerge   she emerges   inside her a womb grows in which a woman can grow & emerge from   she emerges   later the first woman dies   the third woman grows & her womb grows & a woman grows inside her eventually who emerges a womb growing inside her   the second woman will also die   men too are born out of these wombs   men too or parts of men move into these wombs & men & women are born out of them   the third woman will die as did the men & women before her grown out of wombs as will the men & women after her   the fourth woman grows her womb grows inside her as they do & as they sometimes do twin women are born inside her inside her womb & their wombs grow inside them as they grow inside her & eventually they emerge   eventually they marry twin brothers & this is how our story now begins our story of twin women married to twin men who could've grown inside them except they would not have married them then

twin women married twin men   each of them had a womb in which a man or a woman or both could have grown   each of them had a man who was a husband & let a part of him go back inside them to their womb   one gave birth to a man & one gave birth to a woman   that was the only difference you could see between them   the man & the woman were born at the same time on the same day in the same hospital in two different beds where the twin women lay beside each other giving birth to them   & the twin men each passed out cigars to everyone   there was only that one difference between them   one woman had a man who would grow up with no womb inside him out of which another man or woman could emerge but who would send part of himself back into the womb of some other woman causing new men & women to emerge   the other woman had a woman who would grow up her womb growing inside her inside of which other men & women would grow & then emerge

the man who had grown inside the other twin woman married & his woman's womb filled up with a woman & then the woman emerged her womb growing inside her   the woman who had grown inside the other twin woman married & her man moved a part of himself into her womb & her womb filled up with a man & later he emerged   both times the twin men handed out cigars   later these two women's wombs filled with men & women at different times & all these times the twin men handed out cigars   then the twin men & the twin women died   they died all together on the same day & they were still quite young & the fourth woman cried as did the man & the woman grown out of the twin women & the man's wife & the woman's husband & the men & women born out of them & the mother & the father of the twin men & this is how our story of twin men married to twin women ends

later the fourth woman dies   the women grown out of the womb of the woman who grew inside the one twin woman & the women grown out of the womb of the woman married to the man who grew inside the other twin woman gave birth to many other men & women who grew up inside them & then emerged   eventually the man & the woman who grew up inside the twin women died & eventually the men & women who grew up inside them & their women died & eventually after giving birth to other men & women the men & women they had given birth to died & eventually everybody dies after giving birth to everybody else & this is the way it is eventually

THREE WESTERN TALES 1967–1976
for my father

The True Eventual Story of Billy the Kid

this is the true eventual story of billy the kid. it is not the story as he told it for he did not tell it to me. he told it to others who wrote it down, but not correctly. there is no true eventual story but this one. had he told it to me i would have written a different one. i could not write the true one had he told it to me.

this is the true eventual story of the place in which billy died. dead, he let others write his story, the untrue one. this is the true story of billy & the town in which he died & why he was called a kid and why he died. eventually all other stories will appear untrue beside this one.

1 THE KID

billy was born with a short dick but they did not call him richard.

billy might've grown up in a town or a city. it does not matter. the true story is that billy grew & his dick didn't. sometimes he called it a penis or a prick but still it didn't grow. as he grew he called others the same thing & their pricks & penises were big & heavy as dictionaries but his dick remained – short for richard.

billy was not fast with words so he became fast with a gun. they called him the kid so he became faster & meaner. they called him the kid because he was younger & meaner & had a shorter dick.

could they have called him instead billy the man or bloody bonney? would he have bothered having a faster gun? who can tell. the true eventual story is billy became the faster gun. that is his story.

2 HISTORY

history says that billy the kid was a coward. the true eventual story is that billy the kid is dead or he'd probably shoot history in the balls. history always stands back calling people cowards or failures.

legend says that billy the kid was a hero who liked to screw. the true eventual story is that were billy the kid alive he'd probably take legend out for a drink, match off in the bathroom, then blow him full of holes. legend always has a bigger dick than history & history has a bigger dick than billy had.

rumour has it that billy the kid never died. rumour is billy the kid. he never gets anywhere, being too short-lived.

3 THE TOWN

the town in which billy the kid died is the town in which billy the kid killed his first man. he shot him in the guts & they spilled out onto the street like bad conversation. billy did not stand around & talk. he could not be bothered.

the true eventual story is that the man billy killed had a bigger dick. billy was a bad shot & hit him in the guts. this bothered billy. he went out into the back yard & practiced for months. then he went and shot the dick off everyone in sight.

the sheriff of the town said billy, billy why you such a bad boy. and billy said sheriff i'm sick of being the kid in this place. the sheriff was understanding. the sheriff had a short dick too, which was why he was sheriff & not out robbing banks. these things affect people differently.

the true eventual story is billy & the sheriff were friends. if they had been more aware they would have been lovers. they were not more aware. billy ran around shooting his mouth off, & the dicks off everybody else, & the sheriff stood on the sidelines cheering. this is how law & order came to the old west.

4 WHY

when billy died everyone asked why he'd died. and billy said he was sorry but it was difficult to speak with his mouth full of blood. people kept asking him anyway. billy hated small talk so he closed his eyes & went up to heaven. god said billy why'd you do all those things & billy said god my dick was too short. so god said billy i don't see what you're talking about which made billy mad. if billy had had a gun he'd've shot god full of holes.

the true eventual story is that billy the kid shot it out with himself. there was no one faster. he snuck up on himself & shot himself from behind the grocery store. as he lay dying he said to the sheriff goodbye & the sheriff said goodbye. billy had always been a polite kid. everyone said too bad his dick was so small, he was the true eventual kid.

The Long Weekend of Louis Riel

FRIDAY

louis riel liked back bacon & eggs easy over   nothing's as easy as
it seems tho   when the waitress cracked the eggs open louis came
to his guns blazing   like dissolution   like the fingers of his
hand coming apart as he squeezed the trigger
                                                    this made breakfast
the most difficult meal of the day   lunch was simpler   two
poached eggs & toast with a mug of coffee   he never ate supper
never ate after four in the afternoon spent his time planning freedom
the triumph of the metis over the whiteman

SATURDAY

louis felt depressed   when he got up he sat down & wrote a letter
to the english   there was no use waiting for a reply

         it came   hey gabriel look at this shouted louis a letter
from those crazy english   they both laughed & went off to have
breakfast
         that morning there was no bacon to fry   its those damn
englishers said gabriel those damn whitemen theyre sitting up in all
night diners staging a food blockade   louis was watching the wait-
ress's hands as she flipped the pancakes spun the pizza dough kneaded
the rising bread & didnt hear him   its as canadian as genocide
thot gabriel

SUNDAY

the white boys were hanging around the local bar feeling guilty looking
for someone to put it on   man its the blacks said billie its what
weve done to the blacks   hell said george what about the japanese
      but johnny said naw its what weve done to the indians

outside in
the rain louis was dying   its always these damn white boys writing
my story these same stupid fuckers that put me down try to make a
myth out of me   they sit at counters scribbling their plays on
napkins their poems on their sleeves & never see me
                                                    hell said george
its the perfect image the perfect metaphor   he's a symbol said
johnny   but he's dead thot billie but didn't say it out loud
        theyre crazy these white boys said louis riel

MONDAY

they killed louis riel & by monday they were feeling guilty   maybe
we shouldn't have done it said the mounties as they sat down to break-
fast   louis rolled over in his grave & sighed   its not enough
they take your life away with a gun they have to take it away with their
pens   in the distance he could hear the writers scratching louder
& louder   i'm getting sick of being dished up again & again like
so many slabs of back bacon he said   i don't think we should've
done it said the mounties again reaching for the toast & marmalade
        louis clawed his way thru the rotting wood of his coffin & strug-
gled up thru the damp clay onto the ground   they can write down
all they want now he said they'll never find me   the mounties
were eating with their mouths open & couldn't hear him   louis
dusted the dirt off his rotting flesh & began walking   when he
came to gabriel's grave he tapped on the tombstone & said come on
gabriel its time we were leaving & the two of them walked off into the
sunset like a kodachrome postcard from the hudson bay

Two Heroes

1

In the back garden two men sit. They are talking with one another very slowly. Around them things are growing they are not conscious of. They are only conscious of each other in a dim way, enough to say that this is the person they are talking to. Much of it appears a monologue to us as we approach them over the wide lawn, thru the bower of trees, sit down between them on the damp grass & prepare to listen. There is nothing left to listen to. They have ceased speaking just as we appeared. They have finally reached an end to their conversation.

2

Once a long time ago they talked more easily. Once a long time ago the whole thing flowed. They were young men then. They had gone west at fifteen to fight in the metis uprising, urged on by accounts they read in the papers, & they would talk then as if they were conscious of future greatness, made copies of the letters they mailed home, prepared a diary, talked, endlessly & fluently, talked to whoever'd listen, of what they'd done, what they planned to do, but i did not know them then, never heard them, can only write of what i learned second hand.

3

When the fight was over & Riel was dead & Dumont had fled into the states, they went home again & became bored. They would sit up nights talking about how grand it had been when they were fighting the half breeds & reread their diaries & dreamed of somehow being great again.

When the Boer War began they went to Africa to fight there & oh it was great & yes they kept their journals up to date & made more copies of letters that they mailed home, tying up their journals & letters as they were done, tying them up in blue ribbons they had brought along expressly for that purpose, placing them inside waterproof tin boxes, locking the locks & hiding the keys. They were very happy then. If you had asked them they would not have said it was the killing but rather the war for, as they were fond of saying, it was thru war a man discovered himself, adventuring, doing heroic things as everything they'd read had always taught them.

Their friends stayed home of course, working in the stores, helping the cities to grow larger, trying to make the country seem smaller & more capable of taking in in one thought. And they thought of the two of them, off then in Africa, & it was not much different to them from when they'd been out west, Africa & the west being, after all, simply that place they weren't.

4

Time passed. No one heard much from either of them. In GRIP one day appeared a story titled BILLY THE KID & THE CLOCKWORK MAN & it seemed there were things in the story reminded all their friends of both of them, even tho it wasn't signed, & they all read it & talked about it as if the two men had written it, chatting over cigars & brandy, over tea & cakes, as the late afternoon sun streamed thru the windows of their homes on the hill looked down toward the harbour, over the heart of the city, the old village of Yorkville & the annex, the stands of trees still stood there, & wondered aloud if they'd ever see the two of them again, if they would ever receive again those letters, those marvellous tales that so delighted them, & after all it would be very sad if they were dead but then no one had seen them for so long that they were not very real to them.

5

There are some say Billy the Kid never died the story began. There are some say he was too tough to die or too mean, too frightened or too dumb, too smart to lay his life down for such useless dreams of vanity, of temporary fame & satisfaction, that he & Garret were friends after all & Mr. Garret would never do such cruel deeds to anyone as sweet as young William was. I don't know. I read what I read. Most of it's lies. And most of those liars say Billy the Kid died.

There are those who like sequels though. There are those who like the hero to return even if he is a pimply-faced moron who never learned, like most of us, we shoot our mouths off with ease, never care where the words fall, whose skull they split, we're too interested in saying it, in watching our tongues move & our lips flap & Billy & his gun were a lot like that.

When you read a sequel you might learn anything. Of how Pat Garret faked Billy's death, of how the kid went north to Canada or south to Mexico or sailed off to Europe as part of a wild west show, but there's no sequel you'll read again that'll tell you the strange tale of Billy the Kid & the clockwork man.

6

Billy was in love with machines. He loved the smooth click of the hammers when he thumbed his gun, when he oiled & polished it so it pulled just right. He loved to read the fancy catalogues, study the passing trains, & when he met the clockwork man well there was nothing strange about the fact they fell in love at first sight.

It was a strange time in Billy's life. He was thinking a lot about his death & other things. He had this feeling he should get away. And one day, when he was oiling the clockwork man's main spring, Billy made the clockwork man a proposition & the clockwork man said he'd definitely think about it & he did, you could hear his gears whirring all day, &

that night he said to Billy sure kid i'll go to Africa with you & he did, even tho they both felt frightened, worried because they didn't know what'd happen.

When they got to Africa it was strange. It wasn't so much the elephants or lions, the great apes or pygmies, the ant hills that were twenty feet high, it was the way their minds changed, became deranged I suppose, even more than Billy's had always been, so that they began seeing things like their future, a glimpse of how they'd die, & they didn't like it.

7

It was a good story as stories go. Most of their friends when they'd read half-way thru it would pause & wonder which one of them was Billy & which one the clockwork man & each had their own opinion about which of the two men was the bigger punk & which the more mechanical. The women who had known them would smile & say well isn't that just like him or point a finger at some telling sentence & wink & say that's just the way he'd talk.

The mothers of the two men agreed they should never have given them those mechanical banks or shiny watches & would not read much further than this. But the fathers who'd bought them their first guns were proud of them & read it all the way thru to the end even tho they didn't understand it & hoped they'd never have to read it again.

8

The problem with Africa was it was kind of damp & there was no good place where you could buy replacement parts. The clockwork man began to rust. He & the Kid sat up all night talking, trying to figure some way to save the clockwork man's life. There was no way. They were too broke to go back home. Besides they'd already seen that this was how the clockwork man would die.

They got fatalistic. They got cynical & more strange. They took to killing people just to make the pain less that was there between them but people didn't understand. They tried to track them down, to kill them, & they fled, north thru the jungles, being shot at as they went, as they deserved to be, being killers they weren't worth redeeming.

One day they ran out of bullets & that was the end. They tried to strangle a man but it lacked conviction & they just kept heading north, feeling worse & worse, & the men & women pursuing them cursed a lot but gave up finally when the bodies stopped dropping in their path.

The Kid & the clockwork man made it thru to the Sahara with no one on their tracks & lay down on their backs in the sand dunes & gazed up at the stars & fell asleep.

9

When Billy the Kid awoke the clockwork man was very still. There were ants crawling in & out of the rivet holes in his body & a wistful smile on his face. This looks like the end Bill he said & I can't turn to embrace you. Billy wiped away a tear & sighed. The clockwork man was only the second friend he'd ever had.

The clockwork man's rusty tin face was expressionless as he asked you going to head someplace else Bill & Bill shrugged & said i don't really know as there's much place else to go to & the clockwork man sighed then & looked pained as only a clockwork man can as the blowing sand sifted thru the jagged holes in his sides, settling over the gears, stilling them forever.

Goodbye Bill he said. Billy said goodbye & got up & walked away a bit before he'd let himself cry. By the time he'd dried his eyes & looked back the clockwork man was covered in by sand & Billy never did find his body even tho he looked for it.

10

There are strange tales told of Billy the Kid, of what happened next. I heard once he met up with Rimbaud in a bar & started bedding down with him & the gang he'd fallen in with. I don't know. There are a lot of stories one could tell if gossip were the point of it all.

If he went back home he died a quiet old man. If he stayed in Africa he was never heard from again. He's not a fit man to tell a story about. Just a stupid little creep who one time in his life experienced some deep emotion & killed anyone who reminded him of his pain.

And the clockwork man was no better than him. All we can say of him is he was Billy the Kid's friend & tho it's true there's very few can make that claim well there's very few would want to.

11

One year the two men returned. They were both greyer & quiet. They didn't speak much to friends. They'd talk but only if they thot you weren't listening. They had their tin boxes full of diaries, of letters, but then they never showed them, never opened them, never talked about what it was had happened over there between them. They were still the best of friends. They bought a house in the annex & lived together. They opened a small stationer's shop & hired a lady to run it for them & lived off that income. They never wrote again. In their last years, when we came to visit them a lot, they'd stare at my cousins & me & say yes it was grand but & gaze away & not say anything else unless you eavesdropped on the two of them when they were sure you weren't listening. Even then it was only fragmentary sentences they said, random images that grew out of ever more random thots & I was never able, tho I listened often, to draw the whole thing together into any kind of story, any kind of plot, would make the sort of book I longed to write. They died still talking at each other, broken words & scattered images, none of us around, unable to see or hear us if we had been, because of their deafness & their failing sight.

THE BOOK OF DAYS
1966–1971

day 1

someday everything that is begun shall be ended forever as i remember
someone said some thing the same ones always saying those things
they say in vagueness their faces i can't remember even their names
somehow the eyes stick and hold you in fire burning the words crinkle
the page blackening space the words can pass thru into the nothing-
ness

    not as tho there was no hope of which there is plenty but history's
simply the whole thing to be gone over again traces of death can't
even breathe or stop to wishing somehow wishing it were all over
never wanted to start this in the first place sitting here passing the
time he told me get off your ass you cocksucker and write it down all
the time i haven't the inside of another for days barely surfacing to
smile coming back into focus the voice writes it down and i write it
write down to get thru

          a story i never should've begun the whole story
funny the papers fight you they do and no use looking back to the
journal figure it out again said i was lying said of myself i said said it
to me myself i said you're lying trying to lie your way thru again and
it's true i was lying to you now you know just get the whole thing out
of me off my inside me the way it is

        if you could make fiction

           listen
you know it's a simple thing writing the actual thing a somewhere the
way moving down i mean the thots somehow that's where it is

        maybe
i'll tell you about the abortion i was involved in my own history myself
as it were the mirrors no one believes me

      should i tell you a story

        when
you have done the thing you look back and you wonder when you were
doing it wonder how it was done this thing this story words as it were
the piling up of them the counting and why but it's done

once
everything began that was capable of beginning but was cut off
killed   the dream of the child in the plastic bag my own
dream my head bleeding was bled and done over again this story that
child that cannot be borne out of me by reason of my own lack of
reason that is now or will be was when the time comes please
please
understand this i once began as i now begin again that everything is
simply beginning these words again to be somehow rid of them always
as once i was ended i knew i had begun that repetition
this is a story
i began only moments ago and ended as soon as i had begun ended as
soon as my own wish to reveal ended became a running in circles to
seek the son that cannot be mine by reason of that sin
this is the sin
of becoming only those things you allow to begin and then destroy for
fear for reasons of your own lack of being alive destroy what you can
and once destroyed removes those things that were capably begun
oh
god and it's awful isn't it awful sitting to write and you can't write the
story the way you should've when after this only beginning or one
ending and surely of small importance
once upon a time everything
begins becomes and is ended as this is ended or the life of what
could've been life destroyed being part of that which is seen as unbe-
comeable because of those parts of ourselves which were beyond reach
and dead as i said destroyed too long ago to matter but mattering
because it is the story you abort that child's the story and never gets
told
if i say once i mean now i mean i am writing this now and living
it thru again because all things are stories unable to die because of
what i am becoming of words of stories forever untold and nameable
bleeding the tongue and eyes removed from lack of seeing those things
that should've been obvious now destroyed the limp ill-formed body
of could've been it's gone
yes this is a story   no it is not a story it
makes sense   it makes non sense   it makes nothing but the

writer fucked in his own head i am fucked in my own head mirror brain limp eyes

ah and you call yourself name yourself names i am calling always my own reflections myself and in praisings what but the only lonely self never gets told ever the same the lame brained and begun story the whore he should've let go and never himself really let to begin

please god please be to you god to you this story simply to say i'm sorry never should've begun this the way i ended that thing was killing tho my hands never touched it i swear i swear god how i do i do swear i never touched it

who understands? what is at best a question at worst the unnameable moment the hands ache from holding the tense seconds the breath does not release does not carry it held in the chest too long is married to the last moment of seeing that lack of truth you know the meaning of your own lying you did lie you did

me
i was just lying here thot i'd take the day and relax you know i haven't relaxed i thot i'd take the day and try it you know to relax you know i thot i'd try it the irritations you know i mean they do build up you know and i just thot i'd take the day and relax like if that's okay coz if it's not i can simply i mean all you have to do is say so and you do say you did come along and you said c'mon you said to me c'mon you cocksucker get up and write the fucking thing down c'mon confess it you always got to confess it and i do confess you know i do confess i killed it i did kill it didn't even know if it was a girl or a boy i didn't know never saw the body that ugly moment i knew i'd killed it i knew and i never forgave that moment withdrew from it long ago so very far and long ago you came along the road and   told you i was simply relaxing and   you came along and i was simply relaxing you said   you said why are you relaxing i said   i remember the sun was shining i think or it rained   you came along the road   i'd been feeling tired that day and was lying there relaxing as best i could   you said to me haven't you got things you should be doing   i was trying my best   one of those days your whole body aches and   you said i should be writing things down   you came walking down the road rain blowing up over your left shoulder   i hadn't

been able to do a thing that day   i remember it was raining and i'd forgotten my hat   you took off your hat and said good afternoon sir   i bowed   i was very tired   i stood under the trees wait-ing for the storm to break   you passed along the road and smiled in my direction   you didn't speak   i smiled back   it was a bad day   you were walking alone or   i think i remember you looked at me   i'd been tired that day   something had happened but   i was standing alone there under the trees when i thot i saw you

day 2

nothing is ever the same again   what you have done you have done and passed on into the eyes of your only wonder to have been able the whole story ended really nothing and must be ever never the same again   this is important to understand   i told him once in a dream i can't remember i told him never to eat meat when you eat meat i said you eat flesh i told him i didn't like eating in the dream i told him   now i pretend i am someone else and write down stories   what are these things you eat slit belly difficult to hold too slippery no   maybe you always tell lies   maybe the writing is saying i cannot stand it anymore i'll put it down i'll write it down and put that distance between myself and what i can stand can't stand much except distance   move in close to take hold of her writing's lost   the writing's eating your flesh soft teeth sink in nothing really except your brain i meant to say but maybe you never say what you feel no matter how you write maybe no matter how you move anything part of your body you any part piece of you i always a lie until that day   you see there is always a day always one particular day   you get up in the morning and eat   maybe you find a steak in the fridge and you eat   maybe you don't   you get up in the morning and dress   put on the best black shirt and the white tie the hair worn short above the shoulders the black denim trousers and shoes the socks maybe you walk out the door or stand still first to admire the mask you wear   if you eat before leaving it is bacon   you eat bacon and eggs the round yellow   you eat

eggs this morning the bits of bacon the toast the whole plate clean
and you wipe your lips on the napkin and rise   you rise and walk
down the stairs into the street   always there is this one particular
day   there is this day the people smell of meat   you wipe your
lips on your sleeve and rise to descend to the street   always that
one day in particular it is hard to go   there is joy all around you
there is joy   all around you there is meat living and joy in every
pore of it   all around you the meat has mouths and eyes the glis-
tening teeth the meat talks to you   inside you there is only meat
cowering belly soft pressure entrail and sperm whimpering   enter
the street crumpled napkin in hand meat presses against you smiling
        i'd like you to remember this if you can   every day the meat
rises and enters the street to meet you where you stagger out hungry
into the morning air   the meat has hands and touches you says
hello i'd like to know you i would like to you know get to know you
        the meat moves on you moves into the street the crumpled
napkin the dirty sleeve the napkin thrown at your feet catching you
stumble hold it still   and when that day that one particular day
comes you rise in the morning dirty from sleep and dreams of meat
rise & put on your clothes slip out the door and down   no one is
ever the same again   return to that meat you oozed free of
what has been done is done & passes out into the dead eyes of your
only lover's sweet meat

day 3

once i began everything now as now i begin everything once   now
the once that was is no longer as once the now that is could not have
been   all things are infinite and seen in the eye of soon or shall be
being becomeable even tho then it wasn't seen   and what is mean-
ing but saying those things that should be said   what is writing
but telling those things that cannot be told and so are left to be written
as they are and over   is it over   it is not over   nothing is
over until it is written   nothing is written that is understood   it
is only those things that are not understood that are written it is
        only those things that are understood that are over

                                                                    once i was
frightened of flesh as now i no longer can hear my name   people
call me my name i do not know them why   everything seems to
be linked by an and   everything seems to connect in a piling up
        when the flesh piles up you cannot tell what to kiss   when
the flesh piles up you are lost in your own entering your name the
flesh whispers your name you do not know her when her flesh piles
up   writing of flesh the words pile up inside me inside the belly
the prick piles up i feel the flesh near me the heat is on me the hot
feeling in me i cannot breathe   how do you tell her voice from
her hair   how do you know what brushes your tongue your ear
only there is nothing really only her belly moving over you
                                                                    once i
could not have written as i now do not write   i do not write as i
could have written   if i could have written then i would have writ-
ten much as i write now but all things are lost   all things are one
        all things are part of the infinite we are always shattering
every breath is part of the endless   every touch of her breasts and
belly part of the soon to be joining referenceless world amen
praises to her in my hunger   praises to her in my heat   all
motion's part of the moving into her now i could not do once when
the time was on me   the time was on me and nothing in me
all things were like that once
                                        if you are part of the endlessness surely
forgiveness is infinite   surely the infinite endless forgiving wraps
you inside her with love   if there are only these words this page i
am dead   i have been dead a long time
                                                        why is it visions get
shorter and shorter   why is it everything piles up and closes in
        all things are lost as we get older   as we get older we spend
our days seeking what we've lost   when we find what we think
we lost we find we never had it   we find that all we had was the
knowledge of its possibility   that what was lost was that knowledge
of its possibility   and when we find it and find we never had it we
feel a sense of loss   loss at having taken so long to become what
was always becomeable as now we see all things are becomeable if we
only knew   what do we know   we know only our vision is

cloudy as her skin is cloudy   that her skin is cloudy because we
fear to enter into it   she is all things and you are nothing   she
is all that vision is and you see nothing   she is the infinite curving
flesh closes you in screaming   she is the infinite curving flesh
shows you the way free   and you walk her into that vision you
cannot be sure of   into that vision of which you know nothing

if you are nothing what are you   surely writing is nothing
surely writing is saying that nothing   surely writing is saying here
is that nothing this is what it is   out of that nothing all is
created   into that nothing all returns   nothing is simply our
perception of something   nothing is simply our way of saying
something   everything is nothing as everything is something
everything is words we lack the reason for   all reason is nothing
but words piling up against some feeling   all feeling is something
that moves in the nothing and shakes us   we are shaken   it
is something   it's nothing we say it's nothing   all things are
simply a way of returning are what you are

once i was much as i am
now   once i was always thinking i would never be the same
again   there are so many people you could learn to love   so
much flesh you could touch and fondle   your prick is very like
another prick   her cunt's like any other   there is nothing
special in flesh   only you touch it and something's special   you
touch it and the feeling comes   you touch and the humming
moves inside you drives you thinking she is something special and
she is   when i say special i mean i love her   when i say i love
her i mean there is something hums inside me when she comes near
       is she beautiful   i don't know   she is beautiful she is
       always we say we love her and her face changes   always we
say we will care and we do   it ends   it doesn't end   we
move thru our worlds and our worlds touch leaving us the same as we
never were are

so much could be said that is not said   i have said
everything i can say   what are you trying to say   i do not
know what i have said   once i said all the things i just said but
not as clearly   now i say all these things again and am misunder-
stood   i don't understand   why do i say the things i do say

if i started the same way again would it end differently   how
does this story end   if this is a story what have i said then   if
this is a story what story has begun and ended   do you say what
you can always   are there things you can't say   amen
        praise you god for speech   praise you god for eyes   if i
speak now do i lie   if i look now will i see   i have said what i
don't know   i have said what must be said i have said over and
over those things only you said i never said enough times   now
and for all time i have said what must be said   when the flesh
piles up again i won't speak   the flesh piles up again i'll know
i've said my say   it is all said   it is all done & over   is
anything over   praise you god for what is over   praise you
god and be silent amen

day 4

morning evening afternoon   dark skies   outsized windows
such little eyes

i wanted to begin this differently   i can't   i wanted to write
this thing   i couldn't   today it seems everything is broken
        it seems everything is simply words today i wanted to tell you
this story   i wanted to tell you about a friend of mine he was you
know a friend of mine   i wanted to tell you about these friends of
mine their faces   i mean yes that's it really it's their faces they do
i mean somehow yes return again into the mind

what was his name   i don't remember   maybe i do but won't
tell you   this friend he died   did i tell you that   i must've
mentioned it before   i was young then   he was so young then
        yes he died   yes i wanted to tell you then but couldn't
i'm telling you this

i had this friend   i had this friend was called by some name or
other   he couldn't walk   he was five you see & he had to
learn to walk all over again   i wanted to tell you that   this
was a painful thing for him   he was five & he'd been sick & he
had to learn to walk all over again   this can scar you   this

scared me just the thot of it   he was five & forced to learn to walk
all over again

these friends they knew me they knew they didn't know me
maybe they weren't friends   one of them's dead   i never see
that other one the one i referred to then as my friend   i met him
once   he lives quite near me now   we never met then   no
      bright skies outside these tiny doorways   such big eyes

i wanted to end this differently   i can't   i wanted to tell you
these things   i couldn't   today it seems nothing fits   it
seems nothing becomes words today

you wanted to hear this story   you asked me to tell you about
these friends of yours you know who were i mean they were friends of
yours   you wanted to tell me about these friends of yours whose
faces keep returning

what were their names   you don't remember   maybe you do
remember   you won't tell me

these friends die or disappear   did i tell you   you have these
friends   they have names   they die or disappear   so many
of these friends they knew you knew they didn't know you you know

were they really   noon   high sky   outside these eyes these
windows

we wanted to end this differently   we couldn't   we wanted
to tell you these things   we can't   we were friends for so long
      we died   we disappeared   dark skies outside these
bodies outside

day 5

things wear so many faces   touching her skin &   love wears
so many skins   names you cannot name her

this is a story i cannot write   awoke this morning (4 a.m.) scared
& trembling   cold moon over the snow   awoke to no knowl-

edge of what to say

words have so many skins   words so many names

awoke.   morning.   unable.   awoke & moved to write this
down.   speak.   throat.   unable

day 6

lying on the bed head tossed back the eyes do
not open anything but his own face staring in-
to. awaking this morning as any other morning
                        only an hour now the dream had been
he thot his face if there had been another face
                        with him following him even when he
to meet it with. there was no other roll over
                        had awakened. fallen asleep again the
erase it sleep if he only could.
                        dream still with him a fear knowing he
                        was being followed as far as he cared to
                        run. he ran. he had always cared always
                        running. he knew & the knowing was not
                        enough. if enough was anything it was
                        the running despite knowing. he did not
always he thot awaking on a morning he did not
                        know then. he ran.
care to know i have been awaking knowing of things
i did not want to.

                        no place to go. tired. i want to
                        awaken forever. (and this was
                        only one morning. she who was
                        not there was there he had often
                        thot having to think something
                        that it was too true he had never
                        thot and never known her.)

he was always trying to get back there. she had

he did not find it because it was not there.
stood forever in the window becoming a place he re-
he had lost it earlier in a time or place he
turned to as tho to find something.
did not wish to remember. ever.

dear one. cheerless. awaking
this morning bleak &. you are
not here he thot having no
sense of time. you are not here
& have been gone so

he did not know or did not care to know
remembering what had been said so often
only instinct moves me knowing where he said aloud
face to face screaming for the end. here.
her face pressed against his ear. the buildings are
don't begin again she'd say her mouth
formless. i am falling into their forms as if they
swallowing till his voice was barely heard.
were my own form. no they are not my own form. too
no. he had not dreamed it. no. he knew.
possible to become merely trite in the face of the real
no.
world he was falling back into the formlessness he
loved knowing he had not dreamed it. he had dreamed
it.

day 7

surely this time is over as no it is ever this being i do believe now
words are with me again pile together oh i remember you   no i
do not remember you but i do remember   you were there tho this
i do remember as i do remember he used to tell me someone told me
always remember but i don't   he is dead so many years i never
thot he is dead remember   i do remember you are the one i do
remember this moment this morning waking out of that despair i do

remember as it was i saw you yes the sight of you walking toward me
i am glad to be here   so we are here words are here and he is not
here the thot of him here even as you are not words are here   words
are here & i am here & nothing is the same again the words i mean as
they do are not as they are not anything except themselves i mean do
mean themselves   we are they are & that is nothing means nothing
except what it means which is nothing more than that   so words
are here & i am here as the morning dawning i see you again walking
toward me over the words have finally come it's good to see you
        always it seems we are haunted by those things we did or didn't
do as they do become the words you choose you give them weight to
hate yourself with   today the words are nothing   today the
words are here i can do with them as i choose so what if i don't remem-
ber   i will remember even without the words i could remember
yes i could i shall   even watching you now being glad to see you
the words have lost that weight i did give them as i remember every-
thing thru the words remember everyone weighted with words i
do free them use them am i free   yes i feel free of words this
morning free to walk out & meet you smile in your eyes i ask how are
you something you reply   so what if i don't remember i am free
of that weight of words i began from free of memory what i remember
i remember & that is that   i watched you die it was your time i
watched you die lonely i had never felt seeking a voice to speak with
        it is hard to speak   yes it is hard to speak when all the words
are weighted   when all the words are weighted it is hard to speak
        now you are dead & the words are weighted with that grief   it
is not forever   here we are then just the two of us free of words
more free than i can be for years yet you are free   i felt so lonely
then to live thru i somehow free my words of all this weight of memory
to be free   this morning i woke happy sat to write you these words
free for me the first time in weeks i found the words to speak with
        the words slip away i have spoken to you the words free them-
selves of me i remember you i remember   this time is over that
time the words were weighted they are free of me i rearrange them
now they speak to you

Extreme Positions

for Frank & Linda Davey
'a murmur mystery'

S

S S S S
S S S S
S S S S

S S S S S S S
 S S S S S S S
S S S S S S S
 S S S S S S
S S S S S S S
 S S S S S S

```
s s s s s s s s s s s
 s s s s s s s s s s s
s s s s s s s s s s s
 s s s s s s s s s s s
s s s s s s s s s s s
 s s s s s s s s s s s
s s s s s s s s s s s
 s s s s s s s s s s s
s s s s s s s s s s s
```

two
 wives
 wove
two
 waves

twice
 wined
twice
 wifed

two
 waves
 woven

two
 wives

S S S S S S S S S S S S S S S S
 S S S S S S S S S S S S S S S S
S S S S S S S S S S S S S S S S
 S S S S S S S S S S S S S S S S
S S S S S S S S S S S S S S S S
 S S S S S S S S S S S S S S S S
S S S S S S S S S S S S S S S S
 S S S S S S S S S S S S S S S S
S S S S S S S S S S S S S S S S
 S S S S S S S S S S S S S S S S
S S S S S S S S S S S S S S S S
 S S S S S S S S S S S S S S S S
S S S S S S S S S S S S S S S S

s s s s s s s s s s s s s s s s s s s s
s s s s s s s s s s s s s s s s s s s s
s s s s s s s s s s s s s s s s s s s s
s s s s s s s s s s s s s s s s s s s s
s s s s s s s s s s s s s s s s s s s s
s s s s s s s s s s s s s s s s s s s s
s s s s s s s s s s s s s s s s s s s s
s s s s s s s s s s s s s s s s s s s s
s s s s s s s s s s s s s s s s s s s s
s s s s s s s s s s s s s s s s s s s s
s s s s s s s s s s s s s s s s s s s s
s s s s s s s s s s s s s s s s s s s s
s s s s s s s s s s s s s s s s s s s s
s s s s s s s s s s s s s s s s s s s s
s s s s s s s s s s s s s s s s s s s s
s s s s s s s s s s s s s s s s s s s s

1

moon

owl

tree

path or road

stand   ing

tree

tree

tree

birds

                                        moon

            opening

                          hand

landing

star

star

cloud

land

lake

wind

wave

hand

wave

boat

empty

cloud

                      cloud

      cloud

      water

            light

  lake

            tree

                              bush

                  road   me

                                        bush

                        brush

sky

him

step   house

field

window

picture

chair

you

her

eye

moon

                            tree

                                    (adow)

        shh

lake

wave

shore

sky

landing

boat

face

tree

table

chair

empty

2

moving

runs

sitting

scream

crying

laughs

will SHOUT

didn't SHOUT

should SHOUT

can't SHOUT

smile

gestures

stands up

looking

rowing

waves

laughing

smiles

sitting down

sat

cries or
(smile?)
wishes

for
get

for
got

3

yesterday's

colourful

bright

vio
lent
let

swift

bloody

vague

(ness
(ly
))

frighten

startled

(
ah)

(ha
zy)

4

running or sitting or
running while sitting or
running remembering sitting or
yes

   everything at once
altogether
completely tangled up

rowing or sitting or
rowing while sitting or
rowing remembering
no

   everything at once
altogether & forgotten
completely remembered
thrown out

sitting laughing

to sit & laugh

hands

laughing & sitting

seated laughing

hands

sitting & laughing &
laughing & laughing &
laughing & laughing &
seated laughing

         laughing

will shout

(shouts)

didn't shout

(shouted)

can't shout

(wants to shout)

shouts out

(should shout)

shh

wave

wave

wave

boat

wave

wave

wave

wave

happy & sad laughing
remembered laughing hysterical

hysterical sad laughing &
remembered laughing happy

waves

remembered laughing laughing &
sad hysterical happy

remembered & hysterical
laughing laughing
                    happy
                         sad

sitting or standing
standing or
sitting
sitting or
standing
           gestures &

sitting

sitting or
standing or
standing sitting or
sitting standing &

                gestures

the bright boat in
the bright sun on
the bright water in
the bright light in
the eye

in the light
in the water
in the sun
in the boat in
the bright bright bright bright

table fork table plate table knife table

moon or sun

sun's moon

ing sunny &

moon's sun

                                            sun's moon

                                            y sunning &

                                            moon's sun

                                            sun or moon

table plate sun fork table knife plate table moon

shadowy shadow
shadowed shadowing
shadows shade
shedding
        shed
    shys
      shaded
shift

road
lake
road
road
lake
road
road
road
lake
road
road
road
road
lake
rowing

5

why

why not

not why
but why
but not why
not why not but why

why & how

how why

but how
not why

not how but why

how why but not how

how & why

grief

three
            of them
of two of
            us &
two
        them
of us of them

two

three

no
    yes

no
no

    yes
    yes

no
no
no

    yes
    yes
    yes

noyes

noise

an accusation

accusing

(accused)

accustomed as

'unaccustomed as'

accusatory

(a customary)

costumed

    accusing

    consuming

runs

stops

runs & runs

stops

runs & runs & runs

stops

runs & runs & runs & runs

stops

stops

oon

like a lock a lac un like a luck y leak a lack a lake

m

grieving

stands by the lake
sits at the table
walks down the road
runs down the road
gets up from the table
stands in the lake
rows the boat
rows the boa
rows the bo
rows the b
rows the
 ows the
  ws the
   s the
    the
    th
    t

hand

wave

head

wave

hand

wave

wave

wave

head

wave

wave

wave

wave

wave

wave

the moon rises

the moon sets

the sun rises

the sun sets

the moon rises

the sun rises

the moon sets

the sun sets

back.

back & forth &

rocking.

forth &

       rock.

lake.

    ing.

      row.

& back &
forth forth.
back & back &
back & forth &
back.
      back.

6

two
       times
two

              two twos

       time

two twos
to two

                                        (to

everything multiplied
once by itself
multiplied itself by everything
one multiple
everything

     by itself

pardon me pardon
me pardon me

yes

me forgive me
forgive me forgive

yes

you can you
can you can

yes

thank you thank
you thank you

```
        a
   l a k e
        a
   l a n e
        a
   l i n e
        a
   l o n e
```

```
        a
  w  av  e
        a
  weav  e
      e  v  e  ning
                nin  e
  w  av  es
        a
  weav        ing
```

boat afloat
like a lake
like an empty lake
    an empty boat
afloat

                    wave
              wave   wave
          wave   wife   wave
      wave   wave   wave   wave
        wave   wavewave   wave
      wavee   wavweave   wwave
      wave   wawvaeve   wave
  wwavve   wwaavvee   wwavee
      wave   wwaavvee   wave
      waave   wawvaeve   wawe
      wave   wavweave   wave
  wwave   wavewave   wavee
      wave   wave   wave   wave
          wave   wife   wave
              wave   wave
                    wave

waves

S

Still

for Ellie
in the midst of all these years

The front path, marked by the crumbling red bricks half buried in the ground at forty-five degree angles (so that, in the dark, wandering across the wide lawn from the huge oaks that marked the river's course, more than one set of feet had tripped over them, dislodging some of them, breaking the brittle surface of others, scattering bits of burnt red clay among the white pebbles of the path), winds from the wide wooden steps of the house down toward the distant banks of the river. Between the bricks & the lawn in carefully spaced groupings are circular areas of brown earth, where, at indeterminate times to which some seasonal patterning attempts to attach itself, flowers appear. Nearer the river the circular areas become larger, are marked by clusters of boulders in the middle of which dirt has been piled & more flowers planted, again occasionally, in the brief & unpredictable growing seasons of the year. In winter, covered in thick layers of crusted snow, these larger beds merge into the natural slope of the ground as it falls toward the water's frozen edge. The path curves for no visible reason, tracing perhaps an older footpath or animal run or some image, lost now, of how another path once looked, some other yard in which huge willows or maples had forced a more precise construction thru & around them, & from which this path has taken its form, evoking memories, lost now, happy or tragic, or some bittersweet combination of the two, winding & unwinding across the long & sloping yard. Certainly the white pebbles are not as white as they once were, nor as tended, nor are the twisting lines of bricks as complete, and yet, tho years have passed, the path still holds, the white pebbles remain, & the red bricks mark the course all the way from the slippery grass banks of the river to the wide wooden steps of the distant house.

§

'Is this the way you want it to begin?'
　'No.'
'Well then?'
　'You never begin thinking it's going to end. It's not like that.'
'But it is like that this time. Isn't it?'
　'I suppose it is. But that's not what I intended.'
'That doesn't exactly matter now does it?'

'God I'm so sick of you & your "intentions"! The world isn't held together by them! You can't "intend" a relationship with the world, or me, or anyone. You have to have one. It has to exist. All the contradictions intact – but it has to exist.'

'I said I came here with something different in mind.'

'Okay?'

'No. It's what is that counts, what actually happens between us. That's all that's ever mattered to me & and that's all I ask. Let's just deal with what actually happens between us. Not your intentions. Not ever just your intentions.'

§

At night, just beyond the flower beds that edge the verandah, the lights spilling out thru the windows become diffused in such a way that, from the old couch or easy chair, both of which stand just to the left of the door, the beginning of the lawn is barely visible, & the trees, because they grow lower down nearer the river, are invisible – unless the moon is up & the sky exceptionally clear. From the roof of the verandah hang baskets of ivies & ferns that, if a breeze springs up, or a wind, swing back & forth in the dim light, swing back & forth & threaten to fall, threaten to crash against the coco-matting that covers the porch floor, earth & shattered bits of pottery piling on the matted fibre. To the right of the door the old porch swing swings too, & the ivy that covers the front of the house rustles, & the long grass ripples, & the distant indistinguishable leaves of the oaks rustle, faintly, above the almost inaudible sounds of the river. And in the stillness that follows, or that is there in any case, has been there all night or day, has been there all week in the oppressiveness of the summer heat, other sounds distinguish themselves or become garbled, unclear, lost in the dull torpor of the still night air.

§

'I suppose when she died I didn't know what I felt really. That I'd loved her. I knew that. I don't think I ever loved anyone as much as her. But the stupid numbness in myself! I was cracking jokes half an hour later. Then I started reading this journal she had kept & there was her voice speaking & I just started crying & crying. I don't know. It always seems like the really strong emotions have to be built up in some way, as if we have to make the situation extreme before we can actually feel what we feel. Why isn't it enough that it just happens & we feel it? Why do we need some crisis or goddamn drama to make us aware? It sure as hell wasn't that I didn't care about her. But there's that sense that I didn't let her know strongly enough, didn't really get· across to her what she meant to me. You know when that happens you're left with this monstrous feeling that you've neglected someone dreadfully important to you, so important that at times you'd felt you'd rather die than lose them. And you've lost them. You've really lost them. And there you are going on without them. But then comes the even more horrible realization that you've gone on without them for years, that they're as important to you now as they ever were but that at some point you gave up on them. You just fucking gave up! You said somewhere well hell it's all a bit unreal, or overstated or imagined yourself as not being yourself in some way, & you cut off from all that feeling. That's what kills me! No wonder it feels overstated by the time you finally get around to feeling it. God I loved her. I can't even say that strongly enough now. I just went & put that feeling on other people, went & spread it around, diluted it all to hell & called those my "passions." Fuck!'

§

From under the trees by the river's edge, in the dense shadows thrown by the trunks & leaves, the ground rises sharply toward the house, & the path appears & disappears as it makes its way across the broad sweep of the lawn. The verandah seems empty, the angle of the rise making all but the hanging baskets & the front door invisible, & the columns that support the verandah roof, & the half columns that flank the house's main entrance, shine whitely in the late afternoon sun. But the house itself, covered as it is with ivy, appears like an extension of the lawn, like a terminal moraine left behind by some retreating glacier. Yet the glimpsed interior appears warm, almost inviting, some trace of white sheers hung in the windows, too clearly a dwelling, lived in, to be mistaken.

Somewhere behind the house a screen door opens & closes repeatedly, swinging back & forth in the almost non-existent breeze. From this angle the black trunks of the oaks, the white columns of the house, the canopy of leaves surrounding both of them, suggest two clumps of trees, the one clustered near the visible river, the other sending roots down into some hidden source. And of course the invisible world pointed to by the sound of the door's activity is simply the invisible world that any wood suggests – a cool, dark place reached by paths whose entrances appear only at the taking of some optimal position or the conjunction of stellar bodies & specific times of year.

From the shadowed clearings of grass across the long & sunlit lawn to the cool dark interior of the house, the air is a current within which things are carried – sounds, bits of leaf or paper, the spray from the rapids in the river – winding as randomly as any path, everywhere at once & continuous. It is this quality or feeling that most permeates the specific view & gives to each element in it that precise sense of crafted composition.

§

'Did you want something else to drink?'
'No. Thanks anyway. I just don't feel like it.'

'Yourself?'
'I'm fine.'
'Sure.'

'So.'
'Yeah. Funny, I really didn't think this would upset me so much. It's not exactly unexpected.'
'It isn't?'
'Of course not. I'm not an idiot. I can see when things are coming to an end. It's just that saying it out loud somehow makes it so much more upsetting.'

'I really didn't expect it.'
'I know.'
    'I came here intending to talk about where things had come to, where they could go, that sort of conversation. I mean I wasn't looking forward to it but I felt open to possibilities. I find it difficult to even absorb the idea.'
'You did bring it up. It was your suggestion.'
    'I know but ... '

'Here.'
    'Thanks.'

'Christ I just can't believe it.'

'So.'
    'Yeah.'

'Maybe I will have another drink. Can I fix you one too?'
    'That'd be nice.'
'Lemon?'
    'Please.'
'Right.'

'Here.'
    'Thanks.'
'Cheers.'

'It's still not a bad idea.'
    'What's not?'
'Talking. You said you came here to talk about where things had gone to & where they could go to. Let's have the conversation. I'm still interested.'

    'But it's so hard to begin now.'
'So?'

'C'mon. You just begin anywhere. Right?'

'Right.'
'So begin. Anywhere.'

§

The lawn stretches from the river to the house, bounded by those two points, encroached on by the wood near the river's edge, moving out, on the left, toward the still distant field of wheat. The field merges with the horizon, becoming, at its juncture, a shimmering transposition of haze & cloud, air & invisible ears of wheat. The line between the lawn & the field is more distinct. There is a clear edge of turned earth, a marked shift in colour, green to gold, an obvious change in the levels & surfaces of the image. The river, before it disappears behind the trees, winds along the far edge of the wheat field defining its boundary, disappearing, tho we know it is there, marking the end point of the field, an element in the shift & blur of the horizon across the whole width of the wheat's growth. The colour & texture of this huge irregularly shaped area is absolute, consistent even in the patterns the wind makes blowing thru it. And the sun, as it sets below it, adds an element that changes constantly within the fixity of the composition.

§

'Do you remember the afternoon we met? It was here wasn't it? I remember it quite clearly considering how long ago it was. It had been snowing all day, huge flakes that clung to our clothes & turned them white. That was the thing you remarked about when we first saw each other, that we looked like figures made of snow, that we'd both merged with the day.'
    'Romantic thing to say, eh?'
'It was. I was charmed. It was nice to meet someone who had that gift for words & wasn't ashamed to use it. I liked that about you. It wasn't intentions then. You were thinking & seeing things & telling me about them. I liked that. And then we decided to go for a walk.'
    'I remember.'
'We walked for hours, talked, about everything – our families, our various loves, the things that were important to us, silly to us, anything that made some kind of difference to us.'

'You got upset.'

'I was feeling things, stupid. It was such a relief to talk in that way. I was so sick of the lack of connection I'd been experiencing, the emptiness of the relationship I'd just ended. It was a fantastic day.'

'There was an instantly comfortable feeling between us wasn't there? I felt, almost for the first time, certainly for the first time in years, that I could be silent or talk or move back & forth between the two states without feeling self-conscious as I usually did.'

'You had such a lot to say that day.'

'I did, didn't I?'

'No one had ever talked to me about themselves in such detail. I felt you wanted to share everything with me, that you were concerned to hold nothing back because you wanted me to understand you completely.'

'Did you?'

'Of course not. You never can the first time. But you get a sense, an image of what you're reaching for, where it is getting involved might lead to. I liked what I saw. You weren't afraid to show me all your flaws. You really did seem to lack any self-consciousness about them that day. That was the other thing I really liked. It wasn't that old scene of putting your best foot forward in order to impress someone, or your worst foot in order to win their sympathy. It was just you. That's why I fell in love with you. You seemed so perfect & so flawed. So complete.'

'I suppose I was at that moment. Something about you & the day, the way everything seemed to blend into one feeling of continuity. You told me things no one had ever bothered to tell me. Stupid things. What you didn't like about certain kinds of trees. Why you'd collected string as a kid. Absolutely useless information. And then you'd turn around & start talking to me about someone's death, something that had really torn you apart, just like you did here earlier, & everything seemed part of one thing. I loved that. There was no separation anymore. I had a quick sense of how I fit or could fit into your life. That was what I was looking for, someone with that range, who wasn't going to idolize one thing at the expense

of another. I felt a permission from you to be myself, even as you said, with all the contradictions intact. I like the contradictions.'
'I know.'
'I like the fact that the mind's focus can be large & small at the same time, that you can giggle when you're having sex, that life isn't either a comedy or a tragedy but a strange dizzy dance of the two. I really like that.'

'It really was an amazing day.'
'Yes.'

'But so long ago.'
'Yes.'

§

And the moon, when it began to set, added yet another element.

§

'How did that fight begin?'
'Something about a lack of response.'
'To what?'
'I don't really recall.'

'We'd gone to a movie. I didn't like it. You liked it. We started discussing, then arguing, & finally you accused me of being insensitive.'
'Sounds silly.'
'Neither of us was particularly brilliant. I think I said that if that was your idea of sensitivity then I was happy to be insensitive.'
'Deathless!'
'Exactly. Anyway we went to bed not talking & woke up not talking.'
'I don't think I slept actually.'
'By that night we'd "forgotten about it," as they say. But of course neither of us had. We were just a little more careful with our opinions. I don't think we've seen another movie by that director since.'
'It's always humbling to see how one follows thru in one's convictions.'

'It's coming back to me now. I liked his handling of the actors. You said he treated them like mannequins, puppets he could place anything he wanted in the mouths of.'

'Something like that.'

'God I don't even think I'd like the film if I saw it now.'

'It was definitely pretentious but then I didn't really strengthen my argument by getting pretentious in turn.'

'Two wrongs.'

'Right.'

'And that was what that fight was about?'

'Unfortunately.'

'It's completely embarrassing to remember this! What a little intellectual prig I was.'

'We both were.'

'God!'

'Mortifying isn't it?'

'God!'

§

The lawn reaches from the river to the house, edged by the wood near the river's bank, stretching out on the right toward where the river empties into the sea. The sea is hidden below the green horizon line that marks a sudden drop down bluffs toward its rock & driftwood strewn shore: but the sound of waves & the scent in the air mark its presence. The rapids in the river, concealed behind the dense mass of the oaks, are the river's final drop before it slows its movement, mingles & becomes lost in the endless surfaces & depths of the vaster body of water. On long summer afternoons or grey wintry evenings, winds spring up that tease & pummel the wooden verandah, the shuttered windows, the old brick walls of the house.

Along the path to the sea the vast expanse of grass grows coarser & wilder the nearer it comes to the bluff edge. From this perspective the house seems tiny, lost in the middle of the huge lawn, & only the edge of the wheat field peeks out from behind its diminutive bulk. Below the bluff's edge the exposed clay banks fall steeply, & here & there plants cling even tho the face crumbles a little more with each passing year, a little more clay lost in the rain that falls, the snows that melt & run down it to the shore, scoring it, the whole face of the bluff rippled, fluted like the white painted columns of the verandah.

From the shore the sea stretches out toward another horizon line & no other land is visible, no island or imagined continent, simply the water, waves, still again, as the wind rises & drops & the sea moves back & forth against the strewn beach. And from the shore there is no difference between sky & sea, water & air, & everything appears to curve back toward the bluffs, the house, high above, out there.

§

'But you changed somehow!'
'Of course I did. What did you expect? No one remains the same forever.'

'That's not what I'm talking about. We stopped having these kinds of talks, the way we're talking now. You got more introspective, more silent, kept wanting more time to yourself, time of thot you kept saying, & now I feel like a fool for having given it to you.'
'Why? I wasn't lying. I needed that.'
'But look what's happened!'
'What's happened has nothing to do with that!'
'Then what does it have to do with?'

'Maybe you're just a sloppy thinker.'
'Thanks a lot!'
'I'm serious. I keep getting the feeling, actually I've had it for a long time now, that you don't really use the time to think. You just use it to withdraw, to crawl inside yourself & lick your wounds. And if you're crawling around licking your wounds what can I think but that I caused them?'
'The two things aren't connected!'
'So you keep saying! But they must be connected in some way! You sure keep getting into it when I'm around.'

'Something just happened ... that's all.'

'What?'

'It's hard to explain.'

'Well do us a favour & try eh?'

'I can't really pinpoint it. There wasn't just one thing, one big spectacularly bad thing I can blame it on. I wish there had been. That'd make this whole stupid business a lot clearer. It was just one minor episode after another. Like that movie business. Or the sock episode.'

'The sock episode?'

'You remember. I got really upset because you threw out my favourite socks.'

'But no one has favourite socks! They have favourite skirts or shirts but they don't have favourite socks!'

'I did.'

'But how was I to know that?'

'You just shouldn't have touched my stuff.'

'I was trying to do you a goddamn favour! I can't believe this! That's still bugging you after all these years?'

'Not really. But you asked me to tell you what it was, & like I said it wasn't just one thing!'

'Okay. Okay, continue, I'll try not to take it personally. But favourite socks? I mean what are we talking about here?'

'Can I go on?'

'Sorry.'

'I know some of these things seem silly, they seem silly to me too, but they're all that come to mind. I didn't even realize what was happening but I can see now that I've been collecting these little incidents, minute as they are, for years, & in my mind they've all run together to form larger stories, novels even, a body of thot which has as its central premise the notion that if you *really* loved me these sorts of occurrences wouldn't even take place, that I shouldn't *have* to mention them to you, that you should already understand everything about me perfectly if you really loved me &, of course, you can't *really* love me since these things keep happening.'

'That's a hell of a premise & a hell of a big order.'

'I know. But I didn't even realize I was asking you to fill it. And of course on those occasions when you did happen to fill it I took it completely for granted, after all that was the way it was supposed to be, & when you didn't ... well that was a sign & I made a mental note of it & waited for other signs. From my point of view I was being quite generous in delaying my judgments & not jumping to any hasty conclusions.'

'Very magnanimous.'

'I like to make my petty gestures as big as possible. Gives them a certain largeness of spirit.'

'So when did you figure all this out?'

'I don't know if I have yet. This just occurred to me when you asked me what happened. Sounds good tho doesn't it?'

'It makes sense.'

'I can't say I'm proud of my part in creating this situation. But it's the way it happened. That's what you asked for wasn't it? "What actually happened between us." Am I quoting correctly?'

'Yeah, you pass.'

'But these things all seem so silly & petty & inconsequential!'

'They are.'

'And they went on so long!'

'That's the problem really.'

'Why didn't you say anything?'

'I thot I did. Now it's obvious I didn't. And you couldn't read my mind. You couldn't know what I didn't know myself. I fucked up. It's that simple. I fucked up.'

§

Following the curve of the horizon across the field of wheat, far out at the edge, a range of mountains begins, rises above the horizon more & more until, even at such a distance, its peaks begin to dominate the landscape. The wheat field is edged on its right by land that gradually becomes more hilly, rises in gentle steps & curves from the edge of the lawn to the abrupt slopes of the mountains. It is a huge distance but not unimaginable. There is the lawn & the flat scrubby land in between until the hills begin to rise, a vast distance of such hills hidden behind the horizon line, & then the mountains of which only the tips are seen. The river begins in the mountains, makes its way down the sheer rock faces in huge spraying falls of water tumbling into the valleys below, winding its way thru the hills, out, along the farther edge of the wheat field, disappearing behind the trees, flowing over the rapids, slowing, finally, as it nears, enters, the sea. And the lawn, carefully trimmed, marks the left & bottom edges of the wheat field, moves up the right side until it is supplanted by the longer, wilder grass which, side by side with the wheat, continues to the banks of the river. At a distance the wheat & grass merge, in August when the sun burns them both yellow, or in spring when it is all green (tho even then the wheat appears more formal, precise, & the wild grass even wilder, more extreme). From the river's edge, at the boundary between the wheat & the wild grass fields, the house is invisible, the hills closer, more extreme, blocking all but one or two of the peaks from view, & the measured precision of the lawn invisible too. But from the upper windows on the left side of the house the mountains become clearer, more massive & even the river is visible occasionally beyond the wheat & the long grass. And the hills stretch back farther, take on more of their true dimension & width, & the wild grass & the scrub curve on around behind the house, beyond the lawn & the hills take up more & more of the horizon.

§

'Cigarette?'
  'Sure.'
'Light?'
  'Please.'
'Thanks.'

'So what else?'

'Well?'

'It does seem to help if we talk.'
'I know that. I'm trying to get it clear in my mind first.'
   'Okay.'

'I was telling you about how I felt when she died, how it seemed to awaken something in me, or at least made me aware of much she'd meant to me, & how I'd done nothing about that, had let all these other things intervene.'
   'I think that's what tipped me off.'
'What?'
   'When you started to talk about her I realized I'd been doing the same thing with you. In a different way I suppose but the effect was the same.'

   'Sorry. I didn't mean to interrupt.'
'No. That's okay. You just got me thinking about something else.'

'Anyway. I began to think about you & me, how much there had been between us, how much you meant to me. I realized again how I love you & how I haven't said that to you for such a long time. I don't know why. Almost as tho there hadn't been the time or the occasion. Stupid eh? If love-making isn't the occasion what is? But I hadn't. I had to deal with that somehow. I had to understand that. When you said "let's talk" I felt relieved but worried. I know what was on your mind even if you didn't. It seemed like maybe the time had passed me by, that here was another opportunity I'd ... '

'Sorry.'
   'Don't be.'

'It gets a little exaggerated in my mind. Of course I'd said "I love you" lots of times, but I realized so clearly how much of the real strength of the feeling had been missing. Not that I didn't feel it somewhere, but that I didn't let myself feel it with you, treated it all jokingly, that same asinine tendency to crack a joke rather than crack inside.'

'You're not the only one.'

'God don't I know it. I've sure snarled at you enough about that. But so what? It was me this time, or all of those times, and all at once I really felt it, really felt how I'd loved you, still love you, & haven't told you with anything like the real feeling behind it until now.'

'Couple of fools eh?'

'Not a bad description.'

'You always said I had a gift for it.'

'Another cigarette?'

'Sure.'

'Another drink?'

'Great.'

'Well here's to us.'

'Whatever us is at the moment eh?'

'To whatever us is.'

'Cheers.'

§

The lawn surrounds the house. From the river it stretches left & right toward the wheat field & the distant bluff above the sea, sweeping around the house toward the rear, the back yard, stretching out there, farther, so that the house appears to sit in the very centre of the vast expanse of green grass. From the back door a sidewalk composed of perfect squares of paving stone runs straight out to where the lawn ends at the garden. In the garden, at different times of year, flowers grow: azaleas, begonias, chrysanthemums & alyssum, rows of corn & carrots, radishes & lettuce. At the back of the garden is a small orchard

& beyond that the fallow field of wild grass stretches away into the foothills toward the horizon above which the mountain peaks appear, snow capped, & the clouds, the sky. To either side of the path are play areas, the one housing a sand box, the other a set of swings, & from the area beneath the swings the lawn fans out toward the distant line of the bluff, continuing to the right around the house & down as far as the river. Each day the sun rises above the point where the river & sea meet, casting the long shadows of the trees over the lawn, the shadow of the house over the back yard, all these shadows disappearing as the sun moves overhead, reappearing across the front path's white pebbled surface, across the moving face of the river, as the sun sinks, sets below the peaks on the left side of the mountain range. At night only the lights from the windows cast shadows, or the moon, as it moves its trace over the widened circle of moist grass, as it rises & sets & the lights are turned off & on in the barely glimpsed rooms of the house.

§

'What were you just thinking about?'
    'Nothing. Why?'
'It was just this expression that crossed your face.'
    'What expression?'
'Funny. Sad. A mixture of the two.'

    'I was thinking about my little brother for some reason.'
'Which one?'
    'The one who died.'
'Do you remember him?'
    'A bit. He had blond hair, hazel eyes. He looked a lot like my mother.'
'It must have been hard on her.'
    'It was.'

'So what were you thinking about him?'

    'Sorry. What did you just ask me?'
'It's okay. I asked what you were thinking about your brother.'

'Just about him. I was remembering the way he looked, the one clear memory I have of him, playing in the yard. He was wearing overalls & a little plaid shirt.'

'How old?'

'Must've been five. I'm sure the memory's from the day he died. I can't think why else I'd remember this.'

'How did he die?'

'Something fell on him, I can't remember what, I don't think mom ever told me, something heavy tho, & it fractured his skull.'

'I was there that day but I don't have any memory of it. I must've been in a different part of the yard. All I remember is that image of him dressed in those clothes & then later everyone running around very excited & upset.'

'Mom was different after he died. There was always this sadness in her that you couldn't seem to do anything about. We had fun & everything, she was good that way, but there was this sadness in her that you couldn't touch. And she'd talk about him. Not a lot. But she'd remind us of his birthday when it came around, mention him in prayers at Christmas & Easter, things like that.'

'Why were you thinking about him?'

'Eh?'

'Why were you thinking about him?'

'All this talk of death, of things being over I guess. Seems to stir all this up.'

'Where're you going?'

'Just thot I'd open a window.'

'Still thinking about him?'

'Yes.'

'Help to talk some more?'

'Nothing more to say really. Just that image. It makes me feel like crying but I'm not crying am I?'

'It was never one of the things that came easiest to you.'

'I always feel like some ham actor when I start crying. It never flows. You know what I mean?'
'Remember who you're talking to?'
'Right. It's like I'm holding onions under my eyes or something. It always seems to lack conviction.'
'But you're not trying for an acting award! You're just crying.'
'Sometimes I wonder. It's like what you were saying earlier; if the only time I can feel anything is at some extreme moment of crisis then I begin to doubt the validity of it. Maybe I'm making it up.'
'You've got it ass backwards!'
'Thanks for not saying "as usual."'
'It's not actually usual for you. You're a pretty sharp person most of the time. But when it comes to crying you're definitely in reverse gear. For you the very unusualness of the act is what makes you so self-conscious. If you did it more ... '
'I'd get better at it. Right.'
'Well you would.'
'Yeah I suppose I would. It seems like a silly formulation tho.'
'Helps the eye muscles relax.'
'Great. I can see it now. I go for my doctorate in Applied Crying.'
'Could get a dynamite thesis topic going.'
'*Crying In the Middle Ages.*'
'You're just getting silly because the whole idea of crying makes you so uncomfortable. If you feel like crying why not cry? It's human. It's part of how people survive the atrocities & horrors they encounter. It keeps you from becoming numb.'
'*From Numb to Dumb: A Confession.*'
'Your autobiography?'
'Something like that.'
'I'd agree with the title's summation.'
'I have to. I wrote it.'

§

'Kiss me.'

'You didn't ask "why?"'
'I liked your train of thot.'

'An interesting approach to ending a relationship.'
　'You know me. I favour the unorthodox.'
'Mmmm.'

　'So what now?'
'I thot the next step was obvious.'
　'I mean with us!'
'So do I.'
　'Ah.'

'C'mon. You started this. Kiss me.'

　'Nice quotation.'
'A favourite author.'
　'Mmmhmm.'

§

From the river's edge the path of white pebbles curves across the lawn to the verandah's five wooden steps from the foot of which a coco-matting runner follows each angle in the stairs to the top, running across the full width of the porch to end at the front door. The front door is panelled, the eight exact squares forming a larger rectangle of white painted wood, each square clearly framed & then contained again within the larger frame of the full door. To either side stone vases full of flowers sit between the half-columns of white wood & the door frame, & beyond the columns the huge leaded windows open into the diningroom on the left, the livingroom on the right, the two windows framed in their turn by ivy & then the full wooden columns that support the verandah. The door's hinges are brass, & when the brass handle is turned the door swings open, quietly, perfectly balanced, swings open into the cool dark interior of the house. In summer a screen door is attached to the door frame & the interior door left open to allow the air to circulate, the breeze to move across the wide lawn thru the long hallways of the house. In winter the front door is never used, the back one being favoured because of its enclosed mud room, its storage space for boots & coats, those items of clothing which in summer simply hang there, unused, as the front door opens & the summer air circulates, cooling the room & corridors. By the river or among the trees, or even from the edge of the bluff or orchard, the house appears warm in winter, cool in summer, the imagined rooms appropriate to the shift in seasons, & the doors, front & back, open & close, the windows raise & lower, & the house stands there in the middle of the wide yard.

§

'We should've done this a long time ago.'
   'We did.'
'You know what I mean.'
      'But that's the funny thing. We aren't doing anything we didn't do a long time ago. It's just that it was such a long time ago.'

'You're thinking of that first summer.'
      'Yeah. It was great. Things seemed so alive. We had so much to talk about. Plans. Issues. You gave me a lot. There were things we talked about then that completely changed my thinking.'
'Like what?'
      'Philosophies. Points of view. Like that time we met that man who was in such a foul mood & I was just completely judgmental, said what an asshole I thot he was, & you said "Suppose this is the worst day of his life?" It seems so second nature to me now I feel foolish saying it out loud but at the time it was a real revelation.'
'I think we were less afraid in the early days. We didn't spend a lot of time defending our points of view. You wanted to learn. That was how you used to define conversation – as a learning experience.'
      'I was full of those little epigrams wasn't I?'
'But that's exactly what I mean. Now you feel self-conscious about saying it, as tho to be human &, in some way, if you can forgive the expression, "vulnerable," were in itself embarrassing.'

'Why does that word make us wince?'

'Maybe that's part of it. Maybe the language of feeling has become co-opted in some way. It's that same crisis mentality. Everything gets so blown-up, so aggrandized. Maybe if we were all as large as figures on a movie screen & had a full seventy-piece orchestra behind us we could say some of these things & feel we had the proper scale.'

'I know what used to bother me, long before I met you, was the way sitting around with friends we kept having these "serious" talks. There was something quite nuts about it. We were all depressed out of our skulls. We'd talk about real issues but from such a dark brooding point of view that I began to feel we had this really fucked-up idea of what "profound" was all about.'

'Now maybe if we'd put the emphasis on this "found" & not on being so pretentiously "pro" ... '

'That sense of surprise.'

'Something like that.'

'That's what we need isn't it?'

'Surprise?'

'Yes. Tho this has certainly been a find.'

'I wasn't expecting ... any of it.'

'You keep mentioning that.'

'Recapturing my sense of surprise.'

'It is getting cold in here or is it my imagination?'

§

From the threshold a carpet runs down the hall toward the kitchen which occupies the back half of the house. The carpet is patterned, a dark red frieze of leaves, does not cover the floor entirely, an area of polished hardwood flooring left exposed on either side of it. Two sets of french doors open off the hall, the ones to the left into the diningroom, the ones to the right into the livingroom, & to either side of the french doors are old gas fixtures designed to look like candelabra

& now refitted to hold tiny electric lightbulbs in the shape of flames. The walls are panelled in dark oak for half their height & above that a dark red flock leaf-patterned wallpaper has been glued. The left side of the hall has tiny paintings of landscapes in ornate gilt frames spaced evenly along its length between the french door & the end wall of the hall, four of them, their style suggesting they were painted near the turn of the century. The first shows a copse near the edge of a river. The painter has been concerned with the play of light & mist rises from the river giving the scene a blurred formless quality thru which, nonetheless, distinct forms show. The effect is of a landscape viewed at dawn & the trees & grass appear to glisten, forming one continuous surface with the river. The second painting is of a field of wheat, which occupies approximately the bottom third of the canvas above which a clear robin's egg blue has been painted to represent the sky. The technique, the detailed painting of the ears of wheat which because of the use of perspective appear 'closest' in the painting, identifies the period of composition, but the effect, at a distance, is abstract – two bands of colour in bold strokes across the painting surface. The mountains in the third painting seem more traditional; the snow-capped peaks, rugged billowing clouds, the sheer fall of water down the rock face, all these seem familiar. Only along the bottom edge is there some struggle to give the composition a sense of freshness. Here the few visible foothills are rendered in muted browns & golds, abrupt reds, & the mountains appear to form, not from the ground up but from the paint itself, pointing toward some struggle between representational & abstract modes of painting. The fourth painting, like the second, appears utterly abstract when viewed from a distance, & the gold frame, if not gaudy, at least inappropriate. Two almost identical blue rectangles divided by a thin & only slightly darker blue line resolve themselves, as the painting is approached more closely, into an image of the sea on a still day, & the frame, far from being inappropriate, seems to have been built by the painter in order to complete the painting, to surround & permeate the canvas with a glow of golden light. On the right side of the hall a wide, ornately trimmed mirror has been hung & in its surface, depending on the angle, one or more of the paintings can be seen reflected in reverse, & the red flock wallpaper, the dark oak panelling, artificial candelabra, the hinges of the french doors. Below the mirror a small table has been placed upon which a letter lies unopened. In the end wall the door to the kitchen has been hung & the wall has been left blank, except for the panelling & the wallpaper, whereas the front wall has a clothes rack, a place to hang the hats & coats of visitors, & there is a slim black ceramic umbrella stand just to the right of the door as it opens into the hall. Both sets of french doors are closed, but the door to the kitchen lies partially open & at the point where the carpet & the hardwood end the red clay tiles of the kitchen floor can be seen to begin. To the right of the kitchen door a set of stairs rises toward the second floor & on the landing, at the top, the circular legs of a chair are visible.

§

'Did you mean what you said earlier about me & my "intentions"?'
'I guess I did. Yes.'

'I think what I was trying to get at is what we've been talking about here tho. I just want things as they are, the relationship as it is. I can live with that. What drives me crazy is you feeling guilty because you didn't follow thru on your intentions, & me feeling like there's something you've been holding back on me. I can deal with the contradictions, the shifts in mood, but that continuous feeling of pressure! It really does get to me & it's just so completely & utterly unnecessary.'

'I'm not sure I know how to change that.'

'So that's a real problem then.'
'Yeah.'

§

The french doors on the left open onto a polished hardwood floor on top of which no rug has been placed. To the left the large leaded windows look out onto the verandah, the front lawn, the pebbled path that winds toward the distant curve of the river, and to either side of the windows hang dark blue velvet drapes, white sheers hung between them & the wall so that, when pulled, the velvet is protected from the bleaching rays of the sun. Across the top of the window runs a canopy made of the same dark blue velvet as the drapes, & below the window, its back facing the back of the easy chair on the front verandah, a large formal diningroom chair with ornately carved arms has been placed, large potted palms to either side of it. In the wall opposite the french doors, but centred, is a large red brick fireplace with a dark oak mantle, & above it a large mirror hangs, the brass colour of its frame matching the brass screen that has been placed on the hearth in front of the grate to catch straying sparks from the wood or coal fires that burn there. The hearth is composed of the same red clay tiles that cover the kitchen floor, & the brass tongs, the brass-handled poker, the brass shovel for the ashes, have been set on their stand to the right of the screen. To the screen's left is a small brass bin for holding kindling wood & logs, & to the left of the fireplace on the white papered walls, the wallpaper stippled here & there with tiny blue flowers, a large still life has been hung, a painting of a bowl of blue Japanese irises among which clusters of primroses have been arranged. To the right of the fireplace is a window, almost exactly the same dimensions as the still life, thru which the lawn & the distant field of wheat are glimpsed. Along the wall to the right of the french doors a row of four diningroom chairs has been placed, & along the end wall of the room another three, all armless, all part of the same set as the large chair beneath the front window. Neither the wall on the right nor the end wall have pictures hung on them tho both are interrupted by doors, the french ones into the hallways on the right, & a swinging door with large two-way hinges in the end wall which, when open, reveals the kitchen beyond, the red of its floor picking up the red of the hearth, accenting the red brick of the fireplace. To the left of the kitchen door is a sliding hatch thru which food can be passed & under the small window in the fireplace wall a serving table. In the exact centre of the room is a large oak dining table, the ornate carving of its legs matching the design of the diningroom chairs, & in its centre a lace doily on top of which a bowl of purple & blue flowers, primroses & irises, is sitting. Centred directly above the table is a large chandelier made of the same cut glass as the bowl, as the candlestick holders on the fireplace mantle.

The blue velvet curtains are worn. In the chandelier two of the tiny bulbs have burnt out. The light switch for the chandelier is to the left of the door.

§

The french doors on the right open onto a polished hardwood floor on top of which a burnt-orange rug has been placed. To the right the large leaded windows look out onto the verandah, the lawn, the grove of black oaks beyond which the river lies, and to either side of the windows hang dark brown velvet drapes, white sheers hung between them & the wall so that, when pulled, the velvet is protected from the bleaching rays of the sun. Below the window, its back facing the back of the front porch swing, a large brown couch has been placed, & to either side of it small end tables with ash trays & coasters on top of them & underneath each table top racks for magazines. In the wall opposite the french doors, but centred, is a large red brick fireplace with a dark oak mantle, and above it a large portrait of someone, man or woman, difficult to tell because of the darkening of the varnished surface in the centuries since it was painted & because the usual clues, the style in which the hair is arranged, the shape of the lips, have become damaged, bits of paint flaking away, the canvas stained with smoke, at some point, by a fire from which the painting was obviously saved, reframed, but never restored. The frame of the painting has been stained a dark brown to match the mantle, to be compatible with the black iron screen which has been placed on the hearth in front of the grate to catch straying sparks from the wood or coal fires that burn there. The hearth is made of black stone, & the iron tongs, the iron poker, the black tin shovel for the ashes, have been set on their stand to the left of the screen. To the screen's right is a small black bin for holding kindling wood & logs, & to the right of the fireplace another set of leaded windows, framed, once again, by dark brown velvet drapes, & thru which the edge of the bluff can be seen & the clear blue sky above & beyond. Between these windows & the fireplace, & between the fireplace & the bookcase to its left, are equal stretches of white painted wall upon which, above the mantle, their bases level with the bottom of the painting, two light fixtures have been mounted. The oak bookcase fills the rest of the wall, runs completely across the end of the room wrapping around to cover the other wall all the way back to the edge of the french doors. Glass doors, which are now closed, have been built to cover the cases, enclose the books, & the doors have been fitted with locks tho no keys are visible. In front of the fireplace three armchairs have been arranged & a throw rug lies on the floor between them in front of the black stone hearth. There is a small ladder in one corner & some books are piled on top of it. Beams criss-cross the ceiling &, in the nine squares created, small electric light fixtures have been installed. The light switch, which has been flipped up, is mounted in the wall to the right of the door.

§

'I can't seem to stop thinking about her.'
    'Maybe it's only really hitting you now.'
'That's what I think every time I have this reaction. No it's more than that or ... '

'It's more like I can only handle it a bit at a time. Maybe that's the way it is. Maybe you cry a lot & eventually you're actually crying less but each time feels so intense, the feeling of loss is so intense, you don't realize you're getting over it.'
    'Here.'
'Thanks.'

'I just keep thinking how much I loved her & how little I saw of her for so long.'
    'There were reasons for that tho.'
'I know. But if I'd let myself really feel what I felt for her ... '

'Anyway, you know.'
    'Sure.'

'Shouldn't we think about having a bite to eat soon?'
'What time is it?'

'A long time since we last ate. If I have another drink without eating something I'm going to be sick.'
'So let's eat.'

§

The red clay tiles of the kitchen floor extend thru the back door of the house into the mud room. To the left & right of that door cupboards cover the walls from floor to ceiling, cupboards in which dishes, pots & pans, baking supplies, jams & spices & cereals are stored. The cupboards are white, their handles red & the counter, which runs from the hallways door toward the windows in the left wall of the house, has a red top with more cupboards below it & more red handles. Along the counter are arranged tins of flour, rice, raisins & rolled oats. There is a toaster, a number of large cutting boards, a knife holder &, nearest the door, a set of cookbooks. On the wall between the red-topped counter & the full-length wall cupboards is another counter with sinks & a stove which has been built into it. The sinks are in the centre of the counter, the stove to the far left flush against the hallway door wall, a metal hood above it to carry smoke & steam away, & to the right of the sinks a wooden dish rack, a preparation space & yet another cutting board. The window is in the centre of the same wall just above the sinks. Framed by cotton curtains in a calico print, the mountains are visible thru it in their beginning, march away to the right, while between the lawn & the distant peaks the wild rolling scrubland gradually becomes hills. Across the kitchen in the opposite wall is another window curtained in the same fashion, thru which the end of the mountain range is glimpsed, the last straggling peaks, & the distant line of the bluff beyond which the sea, invisible from this angle, beats upon the hidden shore. The left half of the kitchen has a preparation table & the right an old pine one, painted red, around which eight red wooden chairs have been arranged, & on top of which are a butter dish, salt & pepper shakers, a sugar bowl & a napkin holder. The walls & ceiling have been painted the same white as the cupboards & the light fixture in the ceiling is covered with a white globe. Between the hallway door & the right wall of the house is a large white refrigerator which emits a continuous humming, & beyond that the door to the cellar lies open, revealing a steep flight of stairs which disappear into a darkness below.

§

'Then there was that horrible vacation we took together.'
   'A model of non-communication.'
'I think that was probably the worst period in the whole time we've been involved. I'd decided you might have been a sweet person when we met but that living with you was a bit too Jekyll & Hyde for me.'
   'I thot I was being myself.'
'So did I!'
   'Right.'
'What was happening? I've never figured that one out at all.'
   'More of the same I think. I was making these little judgments, acting accordingly, & then congratulating myself on how objective I could remain in emotionally loaded situations.'
'And there I was screaming for a "real" response to *me*.'
   'What is a "real response" anyway?'
'I think in that case you could've defined it as "the one *I'm* looking for!"'
   'I knew what you meant I suppose. You wanted a more feelingful approach from me. But it's funny isn't it the uses of language that go on. I mean I was giving you a "real *good* response."'
'It's all such shorthand! Why couldn't I have said something semi-intelligible like: "Okay, you're being objective here are there any more subjective feelings you could come across with?" I could've at least fished around a little.'
   'You sound too formal tho. I don't think I would've responded any better to that.'
'So what do you think I should've said, Touchy?'
   'How about: "Hi, good looking!"'
'The old sense-of-humour ploy.'
   'Tends to work.'
'But I wasn't in a laughing mood!'
   'Neither of us were.'
'Part of the problem eh?'

'I think so. When I become a sombre, prissy little idiot, the last thing I need is someone coming on in the same way.'

'Thanks a lot!'

'Don't mention it.'

'Want some more salad?'

'Thanks.'

'So it's that same old problem of balance. I don't want to be cracking a bunch of silly jokes when what I feel is something else, but I don't want to be the last word in sombre when what's called for is some humour.'

'It's not always easy to recognize a call for humour, but then separating the counterfeit emotions from the real ones is part of the struggle I guess.'

'Did I get too profound there for a moment?'

'No. I got something stuck in my teeth.'

'Tell the food to watch it. I'm sensitive after all.'

§

The cellar stairs are wooden & open. From the kitchen door a rail runs down the right side & the stairs fall steeply all the way to the dirt floor at the bottom. The cellar is lit by two bulbs that dangle from the ceiling on fraying cords. The furnace is on a raised concrete platform to the right of the stairs, pipes running away from it in all directions. The barely visible walls are piled stone & crumbling mortar, & the wooden columns which must have once supported the two-storey house have been replaced by stacked cinder blocks. On the left side of the stairs is a wooden wall, part of an enclosed storage room in which are kept preserves & a small freezer containing meat & vegetables. The rest of the basement is empty.

§

'What're you thinking?'

'About us.'
　　'Hmmm.'

'I feel totally confused about us now. I figured it was over. I expected it, I didn't expect it, and then when you said it well I felt both relieved & upset. Now I don't know what to think.'

　　'When I try to think of not being with you anymore I just get upset. One could always get by I suppose but I keep wondering what I'm doing ending the relationship.'
'We sure haven't been behaving like it's over.'
　　'We haven't been behaving.'

'Cute.'
　　'A definite failing of mine. I'll try to get more trenchant.'

'So why are we breaking up?'
　　'I don't know.'

　　'Things had become pretty static between us.'
'Yes.'

'But that wasn't the real state of things.'
　　'It just seemed that way you mean.'

'Yes.'

'Which unfortunately does real damage.'

'Do you think real damage has been done?'

'I don't know what to think.'

'I know talking about ending the relationship is completely different from thinking about it. Something happens when you & I start to talk. I get, well, excited. I see possibilities.'

'When we talk this way?'

'Exactly! I don't mean snarling at each other or quoting our little prepared speeches, I mean *talking to each other*.'

'But on the other hand you can't make talking about breaking up the basis for a relationship.'

'Doesn't promote security.'

'No.'

'Confusing.'

'Yeah.'

§

From the hallway a runner of the same dark design & material as the rug follows the stairs up to the second-floor hallway. Between the top of the stairs & the window facing it is an area the width of both the stairwell & the hall that runs beside it, a square area in the corners of which, on either side of the window, two small white wooden chairs have been placed, & between them, under the window, a small circular maple table atop which a bowl of chrysanthemums is resting. White curtains frame the window, & the walls to either side, continuing thru both the second-floor hallways, have been papered in a red rose pattern. The stairwell is enclosed by a dark oak railing & from the window facing the top of the stairs to the turn in the hall, all the way along the long hallway to the front of the house, the dark red carpet continues.

Along the right wall in each hallway, beginning at the doorway to the right of the white chair & ending just before the other wall ends at the window overlooking the front lawn, the same imitation candelabra as on the ground floor have been refitted with small flame-shaped light bulbs. The doorway to the right of the white wooden chair opens into a small bedroom & is the only doorway in that wall. At the juncture with the second hallway the carpet runs left toward the front window & right toward the door to the back balcony. In the long wall that runs from the front of the house to the back are three doors, the one nearest the balcony half-open to reveal a large bathroom, the other two opening into bedrooms. The short wall which runs from the junction of the two hallways to the balcony is bare, while the longer one, ending at the short stretch of black oak balustrade, contains the door to a large bedroom &, between that door & the oak railing, a hanging persian rug. There are no curtains on the window in the balcony door, but the front window, thru which the oaks & the river are glimpsed, is framed by the same white material as the stairwell window.

§

'Sometimes I feel like it's all too much, that I can't live my life at such a level of intensity. I realized that when she died. It's like we spend our lives tuning half of it out, damping down, trying to get some kind of control over what we permit to hit our nervous systems, what we're willing to respond to.'

'Maybe it's a necessary adaptation.'

'Insensitivity as a mutationally developed capability?'

'Not precisely what I was thinking. No it's more like a way of dealing with an environment & a scale we were never equipped to deal with in the first place. It's that old question you & I used to debate. How many people can you really know in a lifetime? Look how many times we've both moved, the people who've come & gone. How many? Hundreds, right? It always amazes me. If I sat down & tried to write a list it feels like it would never end. And when we meet again, after months or years, it's astonishing how much of the original feeling is still intact. And yet there're only a few of those people we really keep in touch with. Do I miss them?

In a way. Could I walk around in a continuous state of missing them? No. I'd be utterly incapacitated if I did.'

'Did I ever tell you about my favourite uncle?'
'I don't know. Tell me again.'
'He was in the war & caught this wasting disease, one of those ones like Parkinson's that causes your body to shake more & more as the years go by. Shortly after the war his wife left him, I don't know why exactly, no one would ever talk about it they were so angry with her. He spent the last twenty years of his life in hospital. It reached the point where he couldn't even talk because the muscles in his jaw & tongue shook so much. He was the kindest man I ever met & the only one of all my uncles who didn't feel uncomfortable around kids, who'd accept us completely on our own terms. He never lost his sense of humour or his sensitivity. You never felt like he was talking down to you or trying to be one of the kids, he was just being himself & you were free to be yourself in return. I remember visiting him in the hospital the year he died. His face lit up when he saw me. He knew who I was & I didn't see him that often because he lived over 500 miles from us. Even tho he couldn't smile with his mouth he smiled. It was completely clear to me. And whenever I think of him I remember his eyes on that day, the complete intelligence in them, & the fact that he wasn't focussing inward on the tragedy of his condition but outward on me & conveying the pleasure he felt in seeing me.'
'It doesn't seem fair does it?'
'It's not really fair or unfair. It's what you were saying earlier – it's the way it was or is. And he astonishes me every time I think of him precisely because all of it, the war, the illness, the loss of a wife whom he'd loved deeply, never seemed to dull him, never became an excuse for him to become insensitive. God knows he would've been utterly justified if he had. But he didn't.'

'So you think it's just excuses then.'
'In a way. That's certainly what it is with me. I feel like I can't take anything more, can't feel anything more than I already feel. It

reaches that point & then I cut off. I might not appear insensitive to someone else but in the terms I've set for myself I know I am. Acceptably insensitive.'

'But then that's what I'm not sure about. Is there a balance point of some kind, some point at which it really does become too much? Torture teaches us there is. But in daily life, just in terms of dealing with this thing we call the real world?'

'And the relationship?'
'You already described it pretty well. I buy myself off with my intentions. I say I need time to think but what happens mostly is I use the time not to think, to try & find a way to shut down. But of course I feel like a good person who's misunderstood because my intentions are always very *very* honorable.'
'Crazy isn't it?'
'I'm beginning to think it's the most common kind.'
'I felt almost exactly what you're talking about when she died. But that's weird isn't it because at the same time as I was feeling like I couldn't feel anything more I was actually feeling more than I had in ages, I was actually getting in touch with what I felt. And not just around her but around you & everyone who's ever meant anything to me.'
'So maybe that's what we mean when we say it's getting too much for us. Maybe at those times we're just beginning to encounter the world as it is.'

§

The window in the small bedroom at the top of the stairs looks out over the back garden, the orchard, the final slope of the mountains toward the sea. The blue in the curtains that frame it is a darker blue than the painted walls, a lighter blue than the flannel bedspread, & on clear days, from certain angles, when only the blue sky fills the window, the whole scene begins to resemble elements in the paintings in the first-floor hall. To the right of the door is a small dresser whose top is covered by a white lace cloth. The mirror attached to the dresser reflects the shelves on the opposite wall on which a collection of small dolls, dressed in various national costumes, is displayed. The bed, pushed tight against the window wall, almost fills the space to the left of the door, leaving a narrow space to the left of it to permit access to the bed & to make it possible to open the closet door. There is a lamp attached to the brass headboard, & above the bed a sewing sampler, letters of the alphabet & a red schoolhouse, has been framed & hung. Between the window & the end wall two shelves run the whole length of the bed & on the shelves books have been haphazardly piled. The old wooden box at the foot of the bed is open & blocks, jigsaw puzzles, & one or two stuffed animals are visible.

§

'It's getting late.'
'I know.'

'I don't want to stop yet tho.'

'Something hot to drink?'
'Tea?'
'Sure.'
'I love you you know.'
'I know.'

§

The two bedrooms on the left side of the house are almost identical. From the doorway of each a window is visible, almost in the centre of the opposite wall, both equipped with blinds & both blinds up. Thru the one the wheat field & the sky above it are visible while thru the other the beginning of the mountain range is seen. To the left of the door in the first bedroom a large window looks out over the roof of the verandah toward the river while in the second bedroom, in the middle of the identically placed wall, is a large painting of an orchard, crudely done, the trees almost childlike in their execution, & the apples painted on in hasty splotches of green & red. To the right of each door, hugging the hallway wall, is a single bed covered in a white bedsheet, the pillows placed on top of the sheets, their cases in each instance having a pattern of red flowers. A black tin light fixture with a small string cord is attached to each bedstead & beside the beds are small night tables on which pitchers of water have been placed. The walls are a uniform white & in the middle of each room a throw rug has been placed, while against the left wall of the house identical small writing desks with identical lamps & chairs are situated directly in front of the windows. There is a closet door in the right wall of the front bedroom, between the foot of the bed & the window wall, while in the second bedroom the door is located on the left between the painting of the orchard & the hall wall. There is a connecting door between the two closets.

§

'Enough milk?'
'Fine.'

'There doesn't seem to be much more to say does there?'
'For the moment.'

'I love you too you know.'
'Yes.'

Thru the large windows in the bedroom on the right side of the house the massed oaks are visible, their huge branches & thick canopies of green leaves, a scattering of acorns on the ground below them, & thru their intertwining limbs occasional glimpses of the white foam & spray of the rapids. On either side of the windows have been hung drapes made of the same dark blue velvet as those on the floor below, & under the window is a large oak desk cut down from an old buffet, the lower cupboards removed & the cut wood stained & varnished to match the natural aging of the rest. On the desk is a large blotter, some dictionaries, a goosenecked lamp, a scattering of file folders, pens &, in front of the desk, a chair similar in design to the ones in the diningroom. Under the window in the wall facing the door is a sewing table with the machine, its cover removed, slightly recessed into the surface so that the cloth to be sewn can slide smoothly over the machine's free arm. Another chair, the same design as the first, sits in front of it. The window is framed by more of the blue drapes & thru the glass, from this angle, the sea is visible beyond the edge of the bluff. On the wall to the left of the door a painting of the house is hung, executed in winter or early spring before the ivy had covered the red brick tho the runners are visible as a network of fine brown lines crisscrossing the entire face of the building. In the painting the front door stands open, the hall within partly visible, the curtains in both the livingroom & diningroom drawn. The flowerbeds in front of the verandah are empty & the effect of the painting is strange, as tho the house had been painted in a deliberately misshapen manner when in fact the style is starkly realistic & highly detailed. The walls of the room have been painted a pastel blue, & the bed, whose head lies against the right wall of the house & on either side of which small night tables are set, is covered with a light blue bedspread atop which four light blue pillows, piled two & two, sit. In the end wall of the room, on the side nearest the hall wall, the closet door lies open & within are glimpsed dresses, suits, dressing gowns & a number of shoes, both men's & women's, in varying styles & colours. The closet appears deep & seems to extend the width of the room. Just inside the hall door, on the left, their backs to the hall wall, are two small easy chairs, a table between them atop which a lamp rests. The lamp is of dark blue ceramic & the shade, chosen to match, is covered in a clear protective plastic. There is a brown carpet covering the floor. On both bedside tables are reading lamps, a few books &, on the one, placed carefully on the side nearest the bed, a small writing pad & a pencil.

§

'I wouldn't want it to be the same & I wouldn't want it to change.'
    'Sounds like a stalemate.'
'Well I wouldn't want it to reach this same point again & yet I like what we have between us.'
    'So you want it as is but more as is than it's been.'
'Something like that.'

    'You think we should stay together then.'
'If we're together yes.'
    'Sounds like a series of bizarre paradoxes.'
'Aren't paradoxes by their nature bizarre?'
    'Not necessarily. But they are paradoxical.'
'Getting cute again.'
    'Sorry. Just can't resist it sometimes. Think of it as my fatal flaw.'
'Don't you think we should stay together?'
    'I do, yeah, but I feel dislocated by everything.'
'The conversation you mean?'
    'What else? Maybe this is part of the problem. The moment I begin to feel more fully what you mean to me I also begin to panic. I can feel it even as we're sitting here talking. The more important you begin to seem to me, the more I acknowledge I love you, the more a feeling of caution begins to grow in me. It's like the two feelings exist in exactly the same place within me, as tho I were thinking & feeling two absolutely contradictory things at exactly the same time, believed both of them to be true, & were trying to act on each of them at the same instant.'

'I want things to continue between us. And I don't want them to change either. But if I get a little glassy-eyed from time to time feel free to holler yoohoo & see if anyone's home inside here. I don't want to make excuses but on the other hand I am the way I am for the moment & it helps if we're both aware of that. Who knows. Maybe it's me. Maybe I'm always going to be this way.'

'Gosh! You mean there's more than one fatal flaw?'

'I'm beginning to sense a bevy of them in there.'

'But I do love you. Just remember that the next time you have to send a search party in to find me.'

'So you've forgiven me for throwing out your favourite socks?'

'Please!'

§

The cast iron bathtub is white & sits under the window in the left wall of the house. The windowblind is up & from this angle the mountains dominate more of the scenery, more of the foothills are glimpsed, & the clouds that gather above the distant peaks appear part of the snow that covers them. The iron taps at the end of the tub have been enamelled white & to the left of the hot water tap has been hung a wire basket in which a used bar of soap rests. A wet orange washcloth has been thrown over the tap & the facecloth & the towels that are hung to the right of the window are the same shade of orange. On the wall to the left of the bathroom door a floor to ceiling mirror is fastened. Some of the silvering has worn off the back of the glass & the reflection of the shelves in the open cupboard on the opposite wall lacks certain items which the shelves contain. To the right of the bathroom door, against the hall wall, its top lying on the tiled floor beside it, is a clothes hamper, out of which towels, socks & underwear spill. In the wall which backs against the balcony, & upon which the cupboard containing the shampoo, toilet paper & extra towels is mounted, there is a white ceramic sink supported by a white ceramic base. To either side of the sink taps are indentations in which bars of soap sit & above the sink a small cabinet whose door contains yet another mirror. The cabinet door opens to the right & at a certain point in its opening arc picks up the reflection of the full-length mirror, which picks up the reflection of the cabinet mirror, which picks up the reflection of the full-length mirror, back & forth, & in which objects multiply & curve away toward some invisible & infinite point. To the left of the sink, its tank against the same wall, the toilet, lid closed, has been fastened to the tile floor. A toilet roll, already half gone, sits on top of the tank. There is a bathmat in front of the tub & an old scale, its weights set at zero, stands at the end of the tub to the left of the window. There is one large light fixture in the white ceiling & the walls are white, the blind white; & the tiles, which cover the bathroom floor, are also white.

§

'Well?'

'I don't feel like stopping yet either.'

'Not a lot else to talk about tho.'
'Didn't I say that a while back?'

'Still involved then?'
    'Still.'
'Lovers?'
    'The works.'
'I like it.'

'Maybe we could make this an annual event.'
    'Breaking up?'
'Seems to help.'
    'Weird but it might do the trick eh?'

'Want a last drink?'
    'Sure.'

    'To us.'
'As is?'
    'As is.'
'Us.'

§

From the banks of the river, the spray from the rapids making the grass & clay slippery, thru the dark shadows beneath the oaks, the ground worn bare in spots, packed hard from the comings & goings of unnumbered feet, an old footpath makes its way to the edge of the lawn. From the mouth of the river where it loses itself in the larger waters, where the rock & debris strewn shore is daily washed by the movement of the waves, another path winds its way up the bluff face, turns left along the top of the bluff, right along the banks of the river, joining the older footpath as it nears the wood or, if the other direction is taken, losing itself miles later in the long grass that overlooks the vast body of the sea. To walk that way, to look first to the right toward the distant horizon of sea & sky, then left toward the house, makes the house appear as it really is: a small two-storey building to which a front verandah & a back balcony have been added; a farmhouse whose barn has long since disappeared; a house built for a different time & thus a different purpose & place. From the bluffs in a direct line with the little orchard another path winds its way toward the house, bypasses it to loop thru the orchard & then, almost as if continuing the back sidewalk, turns to the right & runs straight out toward the middle of the mountain range. Nearing the beginning of the foothills the path winds & twists, making its way thru ravines & gulleys, old river beds, finding its way to the valleys that run into the heart of the mountains. From those same mountains numerous trails snake out & join to make two main ones: the one that finds its way eventually into the orchard & a second one that follows the course of the river, joining, finally, the older path that runs toward the house thru the oak wood. The path to the orchard takes three days by foot, & the one that follows the twists & curves of the river six days, sections of the trail continually being obliterated by collapsing river banks until, finally, as the wheat field is reached, the edges of that more precisely defined area can be followed straight across toward the lawn on the left side of the house, the long grass & wheat making passage easy even tho no path exists. From the edge of the lawn, from the point where the old footpath ends, the white pebbled surface of the winding path that leads to the front door begins. In spring & summer the flowers blooming in the large & small flowerbeds flood the air round the walk with perfume, & the distance from the edge of the lawn to the front verandah is marked by a shifting & blending of fragrance & colour. It is this path & the path from the sea that are favoured in these seasons. Returning from the beach in late July thru the long grass at the bluff's edge, or emerging from the dark wood into the bright sun of the lawn, seeing the house, the house appears larger, more imposing, & the curtained windows seem inviting, mysterious, holding forth a promise that is never articulated. In fall the trails to & from the mountains are more frequented, the mud room providing an area in which to remove boots & coats, a place to deposit the sprays of dying leaves, the bits of fossils. As these routes are travelled, the house disappears then reappears as the path dips, turns, moves in behind the hills & rock outcroppings, out again, up, the roof now visible, then the whole building growing larger or smaller depending on the direction travelled. In winter all this is altered, the paths curving around the house & across the lawn from various directions to reach the back door, the front door ignored again until spring. But in the other three seasons of the year unmarked continuations of all these paths, of other paths only temporarily estab-lished, criss-cross the lawn toward the front verandah, all of them joining at the foot of the verandah stairs. The coco-matting that covers the stair is worn &, in places, the staples have worked loose causing the matting to slide dangerously. The strips covering the porch are worn too & the legs of the couch whose back faces the front railing of the verandah, whose cloth surface is also worn from years of use, first in the livingroom of the house & now, for years, on the front verandah, have worn thru the matting completely & rest on the grey painted floorboards. Only the swinging seat appears new because of the coat of white paint that has been given to it sometime in the past year, sometime in the spring so that the winter snow & frozen air have had no chance yet to chip & crack the surface. But the easy chair & the couch, part of the same set purchased when the house was newer, are comfortable & inviting, make sitting on the porch in the warm summer evenings more pleasurable, & the hanging baskets & stone vases give the porch a garden air that the surrounding flower beds accent. Seen from the foot of the verandah stairs surrounded as they are by the scent of flowers & the distant murmuring of the river, the front door seems less inviting or, more exactly, a thing to be postponed, something to keep closed, sealed, until the moment it is absolutely necessary to use it. As fall turns to winter & the wind from the sea blows in flat across the bluffs, the door is something longed for on returning from skating on the cold ice of the river, longed for precisely because it must remain sealed & the path around the house to the back door seems infinitely long & difficult of access. Running up the path from the river thru the falling rain, reaching the porch, the porch is something to linger on while watching the lightning dance across the sky & strike the distant ground, the front lawn at least three times, the lightning rod on the peak of the house once, & the front door, closed or open, is a source of security, the knowledge that it exists, can be opened, that the house is there & can be entered, reassuring, a presence that embraces by its very familiarity, its nearness &, in reaching for the brass doorknob, turning it, opening the door, a ritual is reenacted whose meaning deepens with each passing year. Pulling the screen door open to turn the handle of the inner door or, the inner door already open or, the screen door not yet in place or already removed & only the one door then to open, crossing the threshold as the door swings inward &, entering the ground floor hallway, turning back to watch the lightning or to close the door quickly because it is winter, because it should not have been opened in the first place, no vestibule to absorb the chill air, or leaving it open because the screen is in place & the house is still hot from the day's accumulations &, standing in the front hallway as the screen door or the front door swings shut, one enters finally, or for the first time, the inside of the house. In the diningroom to the left the table has been set. Viewed thru the french doors the place settings appear, momentarily, as if painted onto the surface of the oak table, the precise arrangement of the blue cloth napkins, blue china plates, silver cutlery to either side, & the blue candles in the cut glass candlestick holders (removed from the mantle & placed in the centre of the table) forming, with the cut glass bowl of white chrysanthemums, a perfect still life. Thru the leaded windows the back of the easy chair is visible, the couch, the white pebbled path winding off between the flowerbeds toward the river. The armchair that had sat in front of the window has been placed in front of one of the place settings & a number of other diningroom chairs have been moved from places against the wall & arranged around the table. The window that looks out on the wheatfield is open & a sliding screen has been placed in it to both hold it open & keep any straying insects out. From the fireplace, thru the french doors in the opposite wall, the front door is visible, the clothes rack, the umbrella stand, the french doors across the hall &, from the one doorway into the other a continuing view of the front lawn is seen thru each succeeding window, each frame (those in the diningroom, the leaded ones in the livingroom, the open doorway of the house in between) recapitulating part of the earlier scene while adding fresh elements to it. In this way the beginning of the woods is first glimpsed from the diningroom (a few trees on the left side of the frame), dominates the whole of the open doorway & then continues to dominate the landscape as seen from the livingroom. A number of magazines lie scattered on the couch to the right as that room is entered: recent numbers of technical journals devoted to particular issues in physics & philosophy, a poetry magazine, a copy of a national gossip monthly & copies of various international news weeklies. The books that were on top of the ladder at the far end of the room have been put away & a number of new volumes have been removed from the shelves & stacked on the floor as if the system by which the books had been arranged is now being reorganized. More volumes are stacked by the easy chairs in front of the fireplace. Along the hall from the front door toward the kitchen nothing has changed. Each painting retains its location, the frames dusted but the arrangement undisturbed, & the letter on the little mail table under the mirror remains unopened & has been joined by a second one. As the door to the kitchen is pushed open, the hinges squeaking as the door swings inward, the hum of the fridge is audible in the hall until the door swings shut again. Here the counter shows signs of food preparation: flour sprinkled on the red top; a cutting board on which a knife rests exactly in the middle of a scattering of small cubes of diced green pepper; a bowl to the right of them containing lettuce, tomatoes, & shredded strips of carrots; in the sink, a number of pots, only their handles visible above the white mound of suds. The preparation table has the largest of the five cutting boards lying in the middle of it & in the middle of the cutting board a roasting chicken has been placed awaiting the toasting of the bread for the stuffing. The chairs around the red table have been pulled back as if in haste & the door to the mud room & the door to the basement are both lying open. From the top of the cellar stairs the basement is too dark to allow any details to be visible & neither the light switch there nor the light switch at the foot of the stairs to the second floor is working. As each of the carpeted steps is climbed, the view that is possible thru the window at the top changes so that first only the sky is visible & then the edge of the bluffs, more & more lawn &, finally, the top stair being reached & the landing stepped onto, the sea beyond all of them. One of the dolls has been removed from the small bedroom & placed in the white wooden chair to the left of the window. The curtains in the small bedroom are drawn, the covers of the bed thrown back, & one of the pillows has fallen off the bed onto the floor & is blocking the door to the closet. The new dolls have been added to the shelves on the right side of the window & the books on the shelves to the left have been rearranged in alphabetical order & stood upright, shiny new blue bookends holding them in place. The mirror in the dresser is tilted so that the back of the top edge is pressing against the wall behind it & the hairline cracks in the painted blue plaster ceiling are reflected. The red carpet in the hall clashes slightly with the blue in the bedroom, more because of the intensity of the pattern than the colour, & here & there has begun to wear thin. In the front bedroom on the left side of the house a suit-case has been thrown on the bed, the contents already taken out & hung behind the closed door of the closet. A dictionary has been borrowed from the bedroom across the hall & placed on the small writing table along with a portable typewriter whose case rests on the floor beside the chair. The window at the front of the house has been thrown open & the fragrances from the various flowerbeds have begun to fill the room & to move thru the open doorway into the hall. The second bedroom is empty. The door to the closet lies open & inside it a number of boxes have been stored, some labelled 'books,' others labelled 'winter clothes,' 'knickknacks,' as if someone were moving or had moved, the process of packing or unpacking not yet finished & the boxes placed here until they could be dealt with. The curtains in the room have been drawn & the light filtering thru them gives the room a quiet, forlorn feeling which the faint perfume of the flowers only intensifies. Across the hall the door to the large bedroom lies open, the window facing it looking out over the bluffs & sea, & in the distance, almost at the very horizon, storm clouds are forming, lightning crackling & dancing on the surface of the distant waves, tho on the lawn around the house the sun is still shining & the breeze has not yet shifted in intensity or direction. The cover on the sewing machine in front of the window has been replaced, even tho the basket which has been brought into the room, & now sits to the left of the sewing machine table, contains a number of torn pieces of clothing, & a package of small white buttons has been placed on the right side of the table. A file folder lies open on the desk to the right of the hallway door, the folder's exposed top sheet appearing to be part of a journal or novel, difficult to determine exactly from such a small fragment, to which a number of revisions have been made, the different dates of the revisions hinted at by the shifting colours & shades of ink. A dictionary lies open on the desk to the left of the folder tho the significance of the pages revealed is not immediately apparent since none of the words defined on those particular pages of the dictionary are written on the exposed page of the folder. There are a number of pens lying to the right of the file folder & a small message pad, devoid of writing, in the surface of which the indecipherable indentations made in the course of writing many now non-existent notes appear. Here too the bed is unmade, the pillows having fallen on the floor & a book, a mystery novel, lies open face down on the rumpled sheets. The closet door is open & a number of items of clothing have fallen on the closet floor. The closet light has also been left on. From the hall window at the front the rapids in the river are clearly visible, the white foam of the water as it smashes against the rocks creating tiny whirlpools, easily seen beyond the leafy green branches of the oaks. Down the hall thru the open door of the bathroom, the clothes hamper is visible to the right of the door, is empty when the top is lifted, when the threshold is crossed the top of the clothes hamper is lifted up, placed on the floor & some article of clothing is or is not dropped into the open basket. The window in the wall opposite the door looks out on the mountains, & the bathtub, wet from recent use, appears as white & cold as the distant peaks. The bathmat is wet & water has pooled on the tiles near the tub & sink. Bits of hair have been caught in both drains & if either set of taps is turned on there is a long wait before hot water comes. The towels which had hung on the wall to the right of the window are now lying in a clump on the floor between the toilet & the end wall. The weights on the scale have been moved, pulling the balancing mechanism down because of the lack of a counter-balance. In the hall the red carpet just outside the door of the bathroom is damp & a number of darker damp spots appear in a semicircle around the larger wet area. Along the hall the door to the upper balcony lies open, the balustrade visible thru the screen door, the orchard beyond, the mountains over which the storm clouds that only a short time ago seemed a safe distance out at sea are now massing. On the inside wall just to the right of the balcony door is the switch which controls the frosted light fixture in the ceiling of the porch and, at night, because of the bug lamp inside it, it casts a muted yellow light. From the hallway of the house looking out onto the balcony a table is visible on the right, two wicker chairs, an ashtray & a deck of cards on the table top &, to the left, thru the thick mesh of the screen door, the porch light not yet on tho the sky is darkening as the storm clouds begin to move closer to the house & the sun to set behind the distant peaks, in the quickening dusk we are aware of two other chairs, another table, & two people who suddenly begin talking.

Afterword

Maps to Another Thinking

Barrie Phillip Nichol (b. September 30, 1944, d. September 25, 1988) dedicated his writing to what he called 'borderblur,' the exploration of the textual possibilities between genre. In the thirty years since bpNichol's death, his poetic work has been extensively reprinted, discussed, and fêted. His concrete poetry, sound poetry, life-long poem; underground comic books, musicals, small-press publishing, and literary commentary continue to have lasting impact on writers and readers. He was also a member of the sound poetry ensemble *The Four Horsemen*. Further, Nichol was known for being a dedicated collaborator, working with countless other writers and illustrators, meaning that we don't even know the full extent of his influence.

In 1970, bpNichol was the subject of Michael Ondaatje's film *Sons of Captain Poetry*. He also appeared in Ron Mann's *Poetry in Motion* and has been the subject of two posthumous biographical films: Elizabeth Yake and Brian Nash's *bp: pushing the boundaries* (1997) and Justin Stephenson's *The Complete Works* (2014). In the 1980s, Nichol created a series of children's books and wrote scripts for *The Raccoons, Fraggle Rock, Blizzard Island, Under the Umbrella Tree, Care Bears,* and *Babar*. His *First Screening* (1984), constructed on an Apple IIe, is considered Canada's first animated computer poem.

Nichol's early 1960s writing was primarily lyric, focussing on his own experience and emotions. After ongoing discomfort with how easily that form of poetry came to him, he began to explore how hand-drawn letters, visuals, comic strips, and other forms of storytelling could challenge his writing process and the limits of genre.

Moving from Vancouver to Toronto in the mid-1960s, Nichol found a community of peers locally, nationally, and internationally who were exploring not only the boundaries of genre and writing, but also sought new ways of organizing their lives. In Toronto's Annex neighbourhood, and in the rural areas surrounding the city, Therafields – a year-round therapeutic community formed around communal living and lay therapy – helped members explore a new vocabulary for open psychotherapeutic communication of trauma and how to move forward toward healing and emotionally honest living. This exploration took place within the framework of rural and urban communal living, communal work efforts, and community construction. Nichol was a lay therapist for Therafields for years, and the writing included in this volume overlaps his time within that organization. The pages of *Nights on Prose Mountain* are populated with Oedipal nightmares, violent sexual and emotional tension and abuse, relationships in crisis, ménages à trois, murder – much of which is described in a way that may be shocking to a twenty-first-century readership. This is the stuff of crisis.

The material in this collection was originally published in six different volumes: *Nights on Prose Mountain* (Ganglia, 1968), *Two Novels* (Coach House Press, 1969, revised 1971), *Craft Dinner* (Aya Press, 1978), *Journal* (Coach House Press, 1978), *Extreme Positions* (Longspoon Press, 1981), and *Still* (Pulp Press, 1984), ranging across the entirety of Nichol's writing career.

But these pages are also filled with prosaic experimentation that belies an openness to explore, to place emotional challenge within a written form which echoes that turmoil. *Nights on Prose Mountain* includes experimentations with the genre conventions of correspondence, stream-of-consciousness, western, romance and detective fiction, sexploitation, and science fiction. His novels formally experimented with collage, minimalism, and fragmentation. Nichol's engagement with fiction was not limited to his own writing – he also, for example, edited John Riddell's collection of experimental short fiction *Criss-Cross: A Text Book of Modern Composition* (1977) and co-edited, with Steve McCaffery, 1976's *The Story So Four*, the fourth in Coach House Press's series of anthologies of experimental contemporary fiction. Nichol's poetry is augmented in the formal innovation of *Nights on Prose Mountain*; each piece includes risk-taking at the level of both content and form.

§

In the preparation of this volume, a series of editorial and design decisions had to be made. The editor has decided to silently correct spelling mistakes and typographic errors found in the original texts, and the typeface has been standardized across the book – but each page presented a series of decisions. Originally typeset in Clarendon with wood-type title pages, *Journal* – like the rest of *Nights on Prose Mountain* – has been re-typeset in Rod McDonald's Goluska typeface, named after typographer, designer, and friend of Coach House Glenn Goluska (1947–2011). Goluska received an American Institute of Graphic Arts (AIGA) Award for *Journal*'s original design in 1979.

The prologue to the book in your hands was originally the untitled prologue to 1978's *Craft Dinner*. It has been moved away from its brethren to the beginning of this volume.

Nights on Prose Mountain, the edition that lends its name to this collection, was originally published by Nichol's own Ganglia Press in August 1969 as *grOnk*, series 3, number 6. This small, stapled edition, with a full-colour cover by Nichol's colleague bill bissett, consists of prosaic excerpts from Nichol's early, ongoing 'Scraptures' series. The Ganglia edition of *Nights on Prose Mountain* predates Nichol's life-long poem *The Martyrology*, but shares concerns and tone.

Of all of Nichol's prose works, *Two Novels* is the most formally complicated. The first hardcover edition of 1969 was printed in two colours in a limited edition of 300 numbered copies by Coach House Press. *Two Novels* was illustrated with hand-drawn colour images, which, in the first edition, were included in a series of sticker sheets in the centre of the book that required the reader to cut out, lick, and place the illustrations in the designated places. And if this weren't enough to create a logistic challenge, the novels were printed back-to-back, and backwards, meaning that once the reader had finished one novel, she was to flip the book over and start from the other end, with the two novels meeting at the middle. The 1971 revised second edition changed the page size and count and replaced the stickers with colour illustrations. The version found here retains the page lengths of the 1971 edition, but changes the typeface and replaces the colour illustrations with black-and-white versions of the same ones. The line lengths, page breaks, and illustrations provide a number of challenges for the contemporary designer; one can only imagine the challenges in 1969 when the text was published using hand-set lead type.

Craft Dinner was published by Toronto's Aya Press in July 1978 in an edition of 631 copies in three different bindings. Like many of Nichol's books, the original edition of *Craft Dinner* explores the physical possibilities of bookbinding and presentation with a design by Paul Davies, printing and binding created by Tim and Elke Inkster and Séamas McClafferty. Of particular note is *Craft Dinner*'s 'The True Eventual Story of Billy the Kid,' which was originally published as a pamphlet by Barbara Caruso's Weed / Flower Press in 1970. Nichol received the Governor General's Award for Literary Merit (Poetry or Drama) that year for the publication of four small books: *The Cosmic Chef: An Evening of Concrete* (Oberon Press), *Beach Head* (Runcible Spoon), *Still Water* (Talon Books), and *The True Eventual Story of Billy the Kid*. Nichol remains the only author to receive the Governor General's Award for a micro-press edition. Nichol's GG Award was not met with universal excitement. On June 10th and 29th, 1971, Members of Parliament Mac McCutcheon and Wally Nesbitt argued in Canada's Parliament that *The True Eventual Story of Billy the Kid* was 'rude,' 'pornographic,' 'an affront to decency,' and a 'discouragement to serious literary effort' and encouraged the government to institute personnel changes at the Canada Council to prevent 'future scandalous, ridiculous, and outright silly awards.' The House of Commons did not agree with McCutcheon and Nesbitt's proposal.

Extreme Positions extends Nichol's use of minimalism and concrete poetry (most specifically in his 1970 boxed edition *Still Water*) into a minimalist 'murmur mystery.' In a 1976 interview with Caroline Bayard and Jack David, Nichol stated that 'publishers never seem to like it – they can't get into it. It's six chapters long. It's a murder novel – well, it's actually a ménage à trois. This guy has two wives and he murders both of them. It's quite linear.' *Extreme Positions* was eventually published in 1981 by Edmonton's Longspoon Press. The lake-blue ink of the original edition has been re-typeset in Goluska while maintaining the poetic page arrangements and page breaks. Within *Extreme Positions* – and operating as a portion of the narrative – is one of Nichol's most famous poems, 'a / lake / a / lane / a / line / a / lone,' which has since been carved into the concrete in capital letters by David B. Smith on what is now bpNichol Lane behind Coach House Books. Rubbings of this engraving feature on the cover of this edition, in a design by Justin Stephenson.

Originally published in 1983 by Vancouver's Pulp Press as the winner of the 5th International 3-Day Novel-Writing contest – which can date the text's composition to Labour Day Weekend, 1982 – *Still's* quiet, deliberate tone alternates between *nouveau-roman*-like descriptions of setting and dialogue between a pair of unnamed, undescribed, ungendered lovers.

The editorial and design changes necessitated in the creation of this collection present these texts in a way that suggest but don't precisely echo the original editions – what is here is a map of potentiality; by standardizing the presentation, *Nights on Prose Mountain* shifts Nichol's intention. Seek out the original editions to see how Nichol explored content and form, design and publishing – explore how page size, paper type, binding, ink colour, and typography each added to a sensory new fiction.

Derek Beaulieu
September 2018

Permissions

Two Novels: Andy and For Jesus Lunatick (1971) and *Journal* (1978) are reprinted with permission of Coach House Press/Books.

Craft Dinner (1978) is reprinted with permission of Aya Press (later The Mercury Press).

Extreme Positions (1981) is reprinted with permission of Longspoon Press.

Still (1983) is reprinted with permission of Pulp Press (now Arsenal Pulp Press).

All work included with permission of Ellie Nichol on behalf of the bpNichol Estate.

Editor's Acknowledgements

A volume like this comes from a community of conversations.

Thanks, of course, to everyone at the Coach House (Stan Bevington, Ricky Lima, Jessica Rattray, Rick/Simon, and Romanne Walker) for the ongoing efforts and dedication in producing books that fuel the conversation and challenge the imagination. Both Crystal Sikma and Alana Wilcox were enormously patient and helpful dealing with the intricacies of the edition; it would not have happened without their exacting eyes and enormous patience.

Thanks to Ellie Nichol for granting permission and support to this project.

Thanks to Justin Stephenson for the fabulous cover design.

Thanks to Douglas Barbour, Kristen and Maddie Beaulieu, Ralph and Elaine Beaulieu, Gregory Betts, Christian Bök, Kit Dobson, Lori Emerson, Kyle Flemmer, Kenneth Goldsmith, Helen Hajnoczky, Richard Harrison, Nasser Hussain, Peter Jaeger, Bill Kennedy, Simon Morris, Justine Renault, Jordan Scott, Pratim Sengupta, and Darren Wershler for the generative conversations and assistance along the way.

Thanks also to André Alexis, Levi Bentley, Paul Hegedus, Michael Ondaatje, Tucker Sampson, Aritha van Herk, and Fred Wah for their support.

About the Editor

Derek Beaulieu is the author/editor of over twenty collections of poetry, prose, and criticism, including two volumes of his selected work, *Please No More Poetry: the poetry of derek beaulieu* (2013) and *Konzeptuelle Arbeiten* (2017). His most recent volume of fiction, *a, A Novel*, was published by Paris's Jean Boîte Editions. Beaulieu has exhibited his visual work across Canada, the United States, and Europe and has won multiple awards for his teaching and dedication to students. Derek Beaulieu was the 2014–2016 Poet Laureate of Calgary, Alberta, and holds a PhD in Creative Writing from England's Roehampton University.

About the Author

bpNichol (1944–1988) created a vast and intricate body of work that stretches from *Fraggle Rock* and *The Raccoons* to comic books, from delicate visual poems to a nine-volume, life-long epic. Nichol was awarded the Governor General's Award in 1970 and spent decades exploring the 'borderblur' between image and text, sound, prose, and poetry – including some of the world's first computer-animated poems. In a career known for collaboration and innovation, bpNichol's writing continues to be generative and generous. Nichol's *The Martyrology Books 1&2, The Martyrology Book 3&4, The Martyrology Book 5, The Martyrology Book 6 Books, Gifts: The Martyrology Book(s) 7&, Ad Sanctos: The Martyrology Book 9, zygal: a book of Mysteries and Translations, Konfessions of an Elizabethan Fan Dancer, The Alphabet Game,* and *a book of variations: love – zygal – art facts* all remain in print from Coach House Books.

Typeset in Goluska and Azo Sans

Printed at the Coach House on bpNichol Lane in Toronto, Ontario, on Zephyr Antique Laid paper, which was manufactured, acid-free, in Saint-Jérôme, Quebec, from second-growth forests. This book was printed with vegetable-based ink on a 1973 Heidelberg KORD offset litho press. Its pages were folded on a Baumfolder, gathered by hand, bound on a Sulby Auto-Minabinda and trimmed on a Polar single-knife cutter.

Edited for the press by Derek Beaulieu
Designed by Crystal Sikma
Cover designed by Justin Stephenson

Coach House Books
80 bpNichol Lane
Toronto ON M5S 3J4
Canada

416 979 2217
800 367 6360

mail@chbooks.com
www.chbooks.com

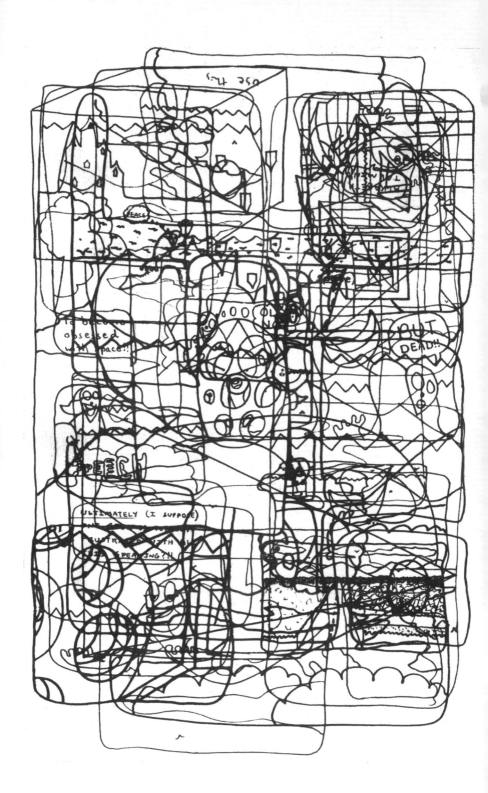